"Do you know what I thought of when I first saw you?" Jordan said. "Summer. You reminded me of summer on Bandora. Gentle mornings, hot afternoons, and the nights—" His finger touched her cheek. "Unbelievable."

Her skin couldn't be throbbing beneath that light touch, Sara thought hazily. It must be her imagination. Then his finger moved slowly down her cheek to the corner of her lips and she gasped. Her lips suddenly felt swollen and her body responded to his touch.

"Summer has many moods but underneath is always the warmth and strength," His finger traveled down her neck to the hollow of her throat. She couldn't breathe, couldn't pull away. "Sunlight. You warmed me." His head bent slowly until his lips hovered over hers. "Heat. You burned me."

He was the one who was burning her, Sara thought. The heat emanating from her body was seeping into her blood, into every muscle, into her bones. She was melting. "Jordan . . ."

"Shh," he murmured, pressing his hand to her chest. "I want to feel your heart beat for me. . . ."

WHAT ARE *LOVESWEPT* ROMANCES?

They are stories of true romance and touching emotion. We believe those two very important ingredients are constants in our highly sensual and very believable stories in the *LOVESWEPT* line. Our goal is to give you, the reader, stories of consistently high quality that may sometimes make you laugh, sometimes make you cry, but are always fresh and creative and contain many delightful surprises within their pages.

Most romance fans read an enormous number of books. Those they truly love, they keep. Others may be traded with friends and soon forgotten. We hope that each *LOVESWEPT* romance will be a treasure—a "keeper." We will always try to publish

LOVE STORIES YOU'LL NEVER FORGET
BY AUTHORS YOU'LL ALWAYS REMEMBER

The Editors

LOVESWEPT® • 257

Iris Johansen
Man From Half Moon Bay

BANTAM BOOKS
TORONTO · NEW YORK · LONDON · SYDNEY · AUCKLAND

MAN FROM HALF MOON BAY
A Bantam Book / May 1988

If you would be interested in receiving protective vinyl
covers for your Loveswept books, please write to this address
for information:

Loveswept
Bantam Books
P.O. Box 985
Hicksville, NY 11802

ISBN 0-553-21896-4

Published simultaneously in the United States and Canada

Bantam Books are published by Bantam Books, a division
of Bantam Doubleday Dell Publishing Group, Inc. Its trademark, consisting of the words "Bantam Books" and the
portrayal of a rooster, is Registered in U.S. Patent and
Trademark Office and in other countries. Marca Registrada.
Bantam Books, 666 Fifth Avenue, New York, New York 10103.

One

The man couldn't have been Jordan.

Sara's grip tightened on the delicate china cup in her hand, her gaze searching the fog-shrouded sidewalk beyond the mullioned windows of the tearoom. It was foolish of her to be so nervous. She had caught only the most fleeting glimpse of a tall man wearing jeans and a white fisherman's sweater before he had disappeared into the fog. She wasn't even sure his hair had been as dark as Jordan's. Yet there had been something about the way he moved. . . . No one had a walk like Jordan's. He moved in a way that was so deceptive at first glance, for it looked lazy, but quite quickly that impression gave way to the truth: He was full of fierce energy. . .leashed. She had watched him stride naked across the room toward her so many times, his muscular thighs rippling with power. . . .

"What's wrong?" Penny Lassiter was frowning at Sara. "You haven't heard a word I've said for the last five minutes."

Sara forced her grasp to loosen on the cup and smiled with an effort. "Sorry. I thought I saw someone I knew." It had to have been her imagination. Sausalito was half a world away from Half Moon Bay and the life she had lived there.

Penny's eyes widened in alarm as her gaze followed Sara's to the window. "Kemp?"

Sara shook her head as she lifted the cup to her lips. "Not Kemp. You're jumping at shadows. Julian Kemp is in New York and no threat to me. It's over, Penny."

"The hell it is." Penny's brown eyes met Sara's as she lit a cigarette. "You were a material witness at Kemp's trial and that slimeball isn't going to forget you. He made threats on your life, dammit."

"That was four months ago and the New York police told us he hasn't given any sign of planning to leave their jurisdiction since Judge Brenlaw declared a mistrial." Sara reached across the table and gave her editor's hand an affectionate squeeze. "I'm not so stupid that I'm not worried, but I can't lock myself in my apartment and never go out. I couldn't live like that. Kemp knows he's being watched by the police around the clock and he'd be a fool to make a move on me."

"Or crazy," Penny said. "And we both know the man is unbalanced. He killed *four* women, and

I'm not going to let you become number five. I've been thinking about it and I've about decided to reassign you to the South Pacific bureau."

"No!" Sara said. "You can't do that. You're overreacting, Penny."

Penny's lips tightened. "I was the one who sent you to New York to cover the finish of that investigation on Kemp, and it's my fault that you were on the spot to witnesss Kemp's attack on the woman. So don't tell me what I can or can't do, Sara."

There was the touch of steel in Penny's voice that broadcast the message she was speaking now as Sara's boss not her friend. Sara experienced a swift rush of panic. No one knew better than she how tough Penny could be when she chose. Penny Lassiter hadn't become the editor of the most prestigious news magazine in the United States at the age of thirty-one by being easily swayed by anything or anyone. Dynamic, intelligent, and charismatic, Penny could also be obstinate as the devil when she made up her mind. But perhaps she hadn't quite made up her mind yet, Sara thought. "I don't want to go back to Sydney."

Penny's expression softened. "Who said anything about Australia? I was thinking about Honolulu. Wouldn't you like to spend six months in the paradise of the Pacific?"

Sara quickly lowered her lashes to hide the relief she felt. Jordan owned a luxury hotel in Honolulu, but he seldom visited it. His brother, Cam, had always handled their properties outside of

Australia. "It's better than Sydney, but I'd probably be bored stiff in your island paradise. I'd rather stay here."

Penny looked down into the amber depths of the tea in her cup. She had been afraid Sara was going to be difficult about this. She had known Sara O'Rourke for more than five years, had been her close friend for about four of those years. She had learned to read Sara pretty well. Not that Sara was difficult to read. She had never tried to be anything but open and honest with everyone.

When Penny had hired her fresh out of college she'd had serious reservations about two of Sara's chief characteristics: her sensitivity and glowing warmth. In Penny's experience, a reporter's sensitivity soon turned to cynicism and warmth to wariness as the years passed. She had thought it likely Sara would become either embittered or so disillusioned she wouldn't last more than six months at *World Report.*

She had been delighted to find herself wrong about Sara, who had gained confidence and strength but never lost her tender qualities. And, indeed, her sensitivity and warmth made her interviews one of the magazine's top features. "Six months will be tolerable. You may even learn how to hula." She crushed her cigarette out in the crystal ashtray on the table. "Maybe by that time the N.Y.P.D. will have enough evidence to file charges on one of the other cases against Kemp on their books."

"But it's not necessary," Sara said urgently. "I

don't want to leave San Franscisco. I like it here and I've made several good friends. I've just finished decorating and moving into my new apartment and I—"

"Honolulu is a long way from Half Moon Bay, Sara," Penny interrupted. "It's not as if I'm sending you into the lion's den. The chances of your running across your ex-husband in Honolulu are extremely slim. If I had a choice, I'd send you to the Paris bureau, but there's no opening there now."

"Jordon has nothing to do with my not wanting to leave San Francisco." Sara met her friend's skeptical gaze and made a face. "All right, I'm not telling the truth. I don't want to see Jordan again. Not yet."

"It's been eighteen months since you left Half Moon Bay," Penny said gently. "You've never flinched at facing up to anything or anyone before, Sara. I think perhaps you've let the image of Jordan Bandor grow too large in your memory. He's only a man."

"Is he?" Sara smiled crookedly. "You've never met him. Jordan is definitely larger than life."

Penny's gaze narrowed on her face. "Are you afraid of him?"

"Of course not. It's just that Jordan . . ." Sara moistened her lips. "I'm not ready to encounter him again. Not yet. Jordan always managed to turn me inside out. He's—" she paused, searching for words—"overpowering."

The description coincided with what Penny had

heard of Jordan Bandor. The Australian hotelier had the reputation of being both ruthless and hard as nails in his business as well as in his personal life. It was a mystery to her that sensible Sara could have been swept off her feet by the man. Of course, Jordan Bandor was fabulously wealthy and Half Moon Bay was reputed to be one of the most beautiful estates in the world, but she doubted that his money would have influenced Sara. Sara had known Jordan only one week before he had managed to persuade her to give up her job with *World Report* and marry him. Nine months later Sara had walked into Penny's office in San Francisco, announced her marriage was over, she was resuming her maiden name, and wanted her old job back. She had never mentioned Jordan Bandor again. Until now.

"Damn, you're actually intimidated by the man and you're no doormat." Penny frowned. "Why?"

"I'm not intimidated. I'm probably giving you the wrong impression. Jordan is brilliant and he can be very charming. You might even admire him. He's just . . . very intense. Probably the most intense man I've ever known."

"Unstable?"

Sara shook her head. "Steady as a rock."

Penny scowled. "I still don't think I'd care for your charming ex-husband."

Sara's gaze returned to the window. "He's not my ex-husband yet, there's some sort of legal delay."

Penny gave a low whistle. "I thought the divorce had gone through."

"Soon. It can't take much longer. I'm sure it's just international red tape." Sara glanced at her wristwatch. "I'd better get going. It's almost four and I have an interview at five with Michael Donovan. He promised me an exclusive about his new science fiction movie." She stood up. "This has been nice, hasn't it? There's something very soothing and old world about taking afternoon tea. If you weren't such a busy lady, I'd suggest we make it a standing date every week." She leaned across the small table and brushed Penny's cheek with her lips. "I'll see you at the office tomorrow."

"Yes, you will." Penny smiled sweetly. "And then we'll sit down and discuss travel arrangements."

She should have realized Penny wouldn't let herself be sidetracked, Sara thought ruefully. "Okay, we'll talk about the possibility of a reassignment."

"Arrangements," Penny repeated firmly. "And remember Mac Devlin's bash tomorrow night. He needs all the support he can get when he tries to wheedle more money out of *World Report*'s board members."

"Mac Devlin needs support like I need that assignment in Honolulu. He'll have them eating out of his hand."

"Maybe, but show up anyway. You don't say no to the publisher, Sara."

"No problem. I'll be there. I like parties." Sara gave her an affectionate smile and walked quickly out of the tearoom.

The fog was becoming worse, wreathing the streets of Sausalito in a blanket of white mist. It was going to be the very devil driving back to the downtown San Francisco hotel where she was to meet the producer. She'd be lucky if she didn't blunder off the blasted bridge.

Sara unlocked the door of her beige Honda and paused a moment to look down the street toward the pier where the man in the white fisherman's sweater had vanished in the mist. Strange what tricks the mind could play. This Kemp business had strained her nerves to the point that it was triggering all sorts of disturbing hallucinations. She smiled ruefully as she remembered that last week she had been sure someone was following her and had called Lieutenant Blaise in a panic to make certain Kemp was still in New York. He had been very patient and reassuring, and even made a special call to the New York police to verify that Kemp was still there. She had felt like a complete idiot.

And thinking that she had caught a glimpse of Jordan had to be her imagination also. He had so dominated her life and her thoughts in the brief period they'd been together that it was probably natural for a stray tendril of memory to creep into her consciousness now and then. But she had neither heard from nor seen Jordan since she had left Half Moon Bay eighteen months ago.

No, it couldn't have been Jordan Bandor who had been standing on the sidewalk outside the tearoom.

•   •   •

Sara drove into the concrete-paved warehouse, parked her Honda, and stepped out of the car. As she slammed the car door, the metallic thud echoed in the empty cavern and caused a shiver to run down her spine. Her footsteps quickened as she hurried toward the freight elevator. Lord, it was dark! Her landlord kept promising he'd install a floodlight, but the single naked bulb hanging over the entrance to the elevator was still the only light. She never liked coming home to this darkness, and tonight it appeared more menacing than usual. The shadows even appeared to move. . . .

"Hello, luv. How's tricks?"

Sara jumped, her gaze leaping to the deep shadows on either side of the freight elevator. Then she relaxed as she recognized the teasing voice. "Cam?"

Cameron Bandor ambled toward her. The light shone on him with cold cruelty as he came within its perimeter. However, it could reveal few flaws in Cam's stunning good looks. It would have been difficult to fault the perfection of classic features, thick tobacco-colored hair with just a hint of a curl, and the loose-limbed grace with which he wore his elegant navy blue suit.

"Lord, Sara, I couldn't believe it when I checked out this address. A *warehouse*, for heaven's sake?" He grimaced as he stopped before her. "I should have known you wouldn't live anywhere that was decently civilized."

"This *is* civilized. In fact, it's very fashionable to have a loft in a warehouse." She hurled herself into his arms and hugged him with all her strength. "Oh, Cam, it's good to see you. I've missed you so."

"And I've missed you." He returned her affectionate hug, brushing her temple with his lips before pushing her away to look down at her. His dark gaze narrowed on the delicate bones of her face and then traveled down to the graceful line of her throat. "You look as gorgeous as ever. Maybe a little too thin— "

"That's fashionable too." She unlocked the gate of the freight elevator. "Come upstairs and have dinner with me. I'll send out for Chinese and we'll talk. Are you going to be in San Francisco for long?"

He followed her into the elevator. "I don't think so. I just flew in from Tahiti this afternoon. It depends on—" He broke off as the freight elevator gave a drunken lurch before slowly beginning its ascent. "What if this ancient monstrosity shorted out? You could starve to death before anyone discovered you were in trouble in this deserted warehouse."

"This elevator works fine, Cam. It's just a little cantankerous." The elevator stopped and Sara opened the gate. "My landlord plans to renovate another area near mine into a nice big apartment. As soon as he finds the financing he'll start, and then I'll have neighbors." She crossed the hall, unlocked and swung open a heavy wooden door, and flipped on the overhead lights. "It's worth putting up with a few inconveniences to have this much space. Do you know how much apartments this size rent for in San Francisco? Rents are out of sight."

"I've heard rumors to that effect." Cam stepped over the threshold and his gaze ran admiringly over the large open expanse decorated in shades of cream, beige, and yellow before lifting to the large skylight overhead. "Nice, Sara. Very nice. It looks like you. All sunlight and warmth."

She gave him a mock curtsy as she closed the door. "I decorated it myself. It took me months to find just the right shade of yellow for the drapes." She strode briskly past the conversation area encircling the prefab fireplace as she headed toward the kitchen area at the far end of the loft. "I'll put on a pot of coffee. Sit down."

"Sara . . ." Cam had followed her and now stood directly behind her at the entranceway to the kitchen. "I can't stay."

She turned to look at him. "You can't?" Her green eyes were suddenly twinkling. "A date so soon?" Cam's list of female conquests was legendary. "It must be one of the flight attendants right? You haven't had time to break out your little black book yet."

"A man of experience always plans ahead," he murmured. "But it's not a date."

"Then why can't you stay?"

"Jordan sent me."

A ripple of shock went through her. She looked away quickly, then back at Cam, and tried to smile. "Since when have you been running errands for Jordan?"

"You know better than that." Cam shrugged. "But he asked me to come and I can't remember a time when Jordan has ever asked me for anything. How the hell could I refuse?"

"He's a hard man to refuse. We both—" She stopped, trying to keep her voice steady. "I think I'll make that coffee anyway. I could use it. This damp fog always creeps into my bones." She took the coffee canister from the shelf. "Is it something to do with the divorce? More papers I have to sign?"

"No."

"I've been expecting to hear any day that—"

"He wants you back, Sara."

She froze in the act of spooning the coffee into the coffeemaker. "What did you say?"

"He wants you to come home with me. He says to tell you things will be . . . different."

She resumed spooning the coffee. Her hands were shaking as she carefully put the scoop down on the counter. She didn't dare pick up the glass coffee carafe yet. In a minute she would have herself fully under control, but she couldn't risk it now. "Is this some kind of joke, Cam?"

"I wish it was." He made a face. "Because I feel awkward as hell doing this. This isn't my kind of scene."

"Then why are you here?"

"I love him," Cam said simply. "Just as you do, Sara."

"I don't—" She stopped and drew a deep breath. "Jordan doesn't understand love. He knows about possession, but he has no conception of any other emotion."

"You don't know him."

She whirled to face Cam, her eyes glittering with tears. "You're right, I don't know him. And he wouldn't let me get to know him if I lived with him for another hundred years. Well, I opted out and I'm staying out. Sex was all Jordan was willing to give me."

"Perhaps he's changed."

She laughed harshly. "Changed? Why should he change? He doesn't need me. Jordan Bandor doesn't really need any woman."

Cam frowned. "Don't talk rot. I've never seen a man as obsessed with a woman as Jordan was with you."

"That doesn't mean he loves me." Her fingers clenched on the edge of the Formica counter. "Sex, Cam."

"Whatever it was, it was enough to keep you both walking around in a daze for nine months." His voice lowered. "Was it so bad, Sara?"

"Not at first." She didn't look at him. "But I couldn't breathe. You saw the way it was. He *smothered* me. He wouldn't let me out of his sight. I had to be Jordan Bandor's woman and nothing else. I couldn't live like that. In the end I would have ended up a spineless robot."

"Sara, he—"

"No! I won't be anyone's possession. Don't you remember that he was even jealous of *you*?"

He nodded. "Jordan wasn't shy about warning me off you. I even thought it was funny at the time. I should have known it wouldn't be quite so amusing for you. I'm sorry, luv, I should have stuck around to make it easier for you."

"How could you? Jordan didn't give me the chance even to see you after those first four months."

"Be fair, Sara. You're speaking as if he kept you a prisoner at Half Moon. I didn't see any locks on the doors."

"No, he didn't lock me up." Suddenly scarlet stung her cheeks and the muscles in her stomach knotted as she remembered the exact methods Jordan had used to keep her helplessly subjugated. No, she mustn't remember any of the things they had done together. Jordan had no power over her body or emotions now. As long as she didn't think of him she was in control. "You're right, I could have left him at any time. It was my decision to stay." She picked up the glass carafe of water and poured it into the coffeemaker without spilling a drop. It was a small victory, but it gave her the confidence to turn and say coolly, "And my decision to leave. I'm not going back to your brother, Cam."

He was silent for a moment. "I didn't think you would, but I had to try." He paused. "He went crazy when he found your note. I haven't seen him that upset since the day—" He broke off. "Men *can* change, you know."

"Not Jordan. He doesn't bend and he doesn't break. Do you think I didn't try?"

"You could try again."

She shook her head. "He's too strong for me. Why do you think I waited to cut and run until he'd gone to Sydney on business? It was hard enough for me to leave then. Jordan has a way of maintaining a sense of presence even when he's miles away."

"He won't give you a divorce, you know. He can keep you entangled in legal folderol for years to come."

"I'm not in any hurry. He'll give up eventually."

"Jordon?" Cam smiled and shook his head. "I told you that you didn't know him." He turned away. "Now that I've done my duty, I'll run along and leave you in peace. Good-bye, luv. I hope the next time we meet we'll be able to just shoot the breeze and catch up on old times."

"I'd like that, Cam," she said softly. "You were the only friend I had at Half Moon, you know."

He glanced over his shoulder. "You didn't consider Jordan your friend?"

She didn't answer.

He shook his head. "He really did make a mess of it, didn't he? I'd have thought he would have been smarter than that. No wonder he's so desperate."

She smiled sadly. "I think you must be mistaken. I've never seen Jordan desperate about anything or anyone. And in spite of your message, I doubt that he's capable of changing."

"No?" Cam opened the door. "Think about it. We both know Jordon is jealous as hell. Unfortunately, that remains the same." He paused. "But he still sent me to you. Maybe he's trying to tell you something."

"Like what?"

"That he knows he has to trust you and come to terms with what you want in a relationship."

"It's too late," she whispered.

Cam's expression reflected genuine regret. "I'm sorry as hell to hear that, but I'll deliver the message." He started for the door.

"Cam."

He stopped. "Yes?"

"Where will you deliver it?" She moistened her lips nervously. "This afternoon I thought I caught a glimpse of Jordan in the street. Later I realized it must have been my imagination but . . . He's not here in San Francisco?"

"I haven't seen him if he is." Something flickered in Cam's face and then was gone. "I was in Papeete when he phoned to ask me to come and see you. I assumed he was calling from Half Moon."

Dizzying relief poured through her. "Yes, of course. I knew I was mistaken."

Cam started to speak, obviously changed his mind, then smiled. "Good-bye, luv, see you next time."

She nodded. "Next time."

The door closed behind him, and Sara let out

her pent-up breath in a rush. How odd to be this tense in Cam's presence when she had always been so comfortable with him. She was still trembling with nerves even though he was no longer there. Lord, why was she lying to herself, she wondered with sudden impatience. It wasn't Cam who was generating this sense of panic. It was Jordan.

Just talking about Jordan had brought back the tempest of emotions he created in her. She felt bewilderment, fear, lust. And it *was* lust, she assured herself frantically. It couldn't be love. During those first heady months of their marriage she had talked herself into believing she loved him, but how could she love a stranger? No, her attachment to Jordan had to be purely sexual. Every woman was entitled to one mad episode in her life, and Sara's had been with Jordan Bandor. Now her months of temporary insanity were behind her—and that was exactly where she wanted them to stay. She had worked too hard to forget Jordan to let Cam's words disturb her equanimity.

She started to reach up into the cabinet for a coffee cup and then changed her mind. She was going to have enough trouble sleeping tonight without loading herself with caffeine. She switched off the coffeemaker and turned away. She would dismiss all thoughts of Jordan and concentrate on—

Eighteen months. Why had he waited eighteen months to contact her and why hadn't he told her he intended to fight the divorce? Why appear out of the blue after all this time? She had thought it odd he hadn't tried to contact her after she left Half Moon but assumed he had been consumed by rage and decided to cut her out of his life. She had witnessed his cold ferocity toward adversaries in business, so she thought it quite likely he would treat her in that same way.

She could feel the tension stiffening her muscles and deliberately drew a deep breath, forcing herself to relax. She'd take a hot shower and go to bed. There would be time enough for typing up her notes on the Donovan interview tomorrow morning. Now she must make sure no thoughts of Jordan penetrated the walls she'd built against him. She would go to sleep and by tomorrow her defenses would be stronger.

It was the tactic she had used during those first weeks after she had left him, and it had worked very well. She had only to live hour by hour and minute by minute. Yes, that was the way to survive. She moved wearily toward the Oriental lattice divider that screened her bedroom and bath from the rest of the loft. She had learned a great deal about surviving in these last months, she thought. Jordan had almost destroyed her as an individual, but she had fought back and was her own person again.

And she was damn well going to stay that way.

Mac Devlin's penthouse apartment was all glittering crystal chandeliers, white and ebony velvet cushioned modern furniture, and open space. At the moment almost every inch of that space was occupied by laughing, talking men and women who were more glittering than the crystal chandeliers. From the doorway Sara's gaze idly searched the crowd. She knew some of the people, but most of them were strangers. Then she caught sight of Kelly and Nick O'Brian across the room talking to Mac and immediately began to work her way toward them. She had gone only a few feet, when Penny appeared at her side.

"You made it." Penny grinned as she took two fluted glasses from the tray of a passing white-coated waiter and handed one to Sara. "Hold on to this. It might be the last drink you'll get before dinner. Mac should have tagged the waiters with fluorescent safety strips. It's almost impossible to find one in this mob."

"Why didn't you suggest it?"

"I haven't been able to get near enough to him even to shout." Penny's gaze flicked over Sara's sleeveless wine-colored velvet gown. "Pretty." She made a face. "But if I had bazooms like Racquel Welch, I wouldn't be wearing that cowl neck. If you've got it, flaunt it, I always say."

"That's what I always say too." Sara's green eyes were twinkling as she turned her back on Penny. "But flaunt it discreetly."

The velvet gown bared her entire back and formed a daring V that ended two inches below her waist.

Penny laughed and shook her head as Sara again

turned to face her. "As your editor, I think I should suggest you get a better dictionary. There's no way that gown could be called discreet." Her smile faded. "I haven't forgotten about Honolulu, by the way. I was yanked into a production meeting this afternoon or I would have pinned you down about—"

"How did you like the Donovan story?"

"The bit about his wife and family was good stuff." Penny frowned. "Quit trying to sidle away from the issue. I'm not about to let you— What's wrong? You look as if someone just hit you in the stomach." Penny turned and followed Sara's gaze across the room to the corner in which Mac was holding court. Her lips pursed in a soundless whistle. "And who could blame you? I feel a little weak-kneed myself. Lord, he's gorgeous. Sort of a cross between Mel Gibson and Brenda Starr's mystery man, isn't he?"

"Yes," Sara said numbly.

Penny took a sip of her drink, her brown eyes narrowed on the tuxedo-clad man in conversation with Mac. "Do you suppose he's a movie star? Who else would have nerve enough to wear a black patch over one eye? He looks like a buccaneer in one of those old Errol Flynn movies."

Sara didn't answer.

"I think I may just gird my loins and try to fight my way over there," Penny murmured. "What a fantastic tush. I've always been a sucker for men with—" She broke off as soon as she turned back and saw Sara's expression, which betrayed not only surprise but panic. "You know him?"

Sara nodded, her gaze never leaving the man with the black eyepatch. "It's Jordan."

Penny uttered a soft curse beneath her breath as she gazed once more at the man across the room. Only yesterday she had been wondering how "sensible" Sara could have been swept off her feet by a hardliner like Jordan Bandor. Now her answer was here before her. He possessed more sexual magnetism than any man Penny had ever seen. He stood a little over six feet but appeared larger. He was all sleek bronze muscle and leashed power, and that tush . . . Penny forced her gaze up to Jordan Bandor's face. The planes and bones were more arresting than conventionally good-looking, but his mouth was beautifully shaped and that damn eyepatch was sexy as the devil. Cripes, no wonder Sara had fallen like a ton of bricks. She didn't know many women who wouldn't have been drawn by Jordan's sex appeal. She took a protective step closer to Sara. "Do you want to leave? I'll make your excuses to Mac."

"No." Sara closed her eyes for the tenth of a second and then opened them and turned to smile at Penny. "I'm all right. It had to happen sometime. I just didn't expect—"

"What the hell is he doing here?" Penny asked fiercely. "Why couldn't he stay on his own side of the world?"

"Jordan doesn't believe in limiting himself. To-day the South Pacific, tomorrow . . . who knows?"

Sara took a quick swallow of champagne. "I imagine we'll learn soon enough why he's here. Jordan isn't in the least Machiavellian. He just sets a goal and blows a path through hell and high water until he gets it."

Penny could believe that as she continued to glare at the man across the room. Jordan gave the impression of total stillness, yet he was exuding a stream of power and energy as he bent his dark head to listen to something Mac was saying. She could feel herself bristling with instinctive defensiveness. "What do you say we get out of here and go to the Top of the Mark for a drink?"

Sara smiled affectionately. "You know Mac would hit the roof if you didn't stay and socialize with all these bigwigs. Stop worrying about me, Penny. You told me yourself yesterday afternoon that I'd have to face him sometime."

But that was before Penny had seen Jordan and gauged his mettle. "I've been known to have a very big mouth. Well, if you won't leave, then let's go beard the Aussie and show him how well you're doing without him."

Sara shook her head. "Thanks for the support, but I don't need you to hold my hand. I'm twenty-seven years old, for heaven's sake. Go do your duty and mingle."

Penny hesitated. "You're sure?"

"I'm fine." Sara lifted her glass to her lips. "I was just surprised. Jordan is—" She inhaled sharply and forgot what she was saying as Jordan looked up and saw her. He didn't change expression, but she could feel the waves of emotion radiating from him across the room and her grasp unconsciously tightened on the fragile stem of her glass. She had forgotten the lightning blue of that glance and how much intensity he could project.

"Sara?"

Penny's concerned voice freed her and Sara tore her gaze away and forced a bright smile. "I'm fine," she repeated. "Beat it."

Penny gazed at her skeptically and then shrugged. "I'll check back with you later." She turned and disappeared into the crowd.

Sara looked down at the clear sparkling liquid in her glass. He would be coming soon. He would be crossing the room, negotiating his way through the crowd that would part instinctively for him. Nothing would stop him or distract him. Soon he would be here beside her.

"Hello, Sara."

Her gaze rose to fasten on his face. Oh, God, she didn't want this. She drew a shaky breath. "What are you doing here?"

"Waiting for you." His lips tightened. "Not that that's anything new. I've been waiting for you for the last eighteen months." His gaze traveled over the delicate planes of her face, lingering on the softness of her mouth and then going to the silver blond of her hair curving beneath her chin in a shining Dutch boy bob. He frowned. "You've cut your hair. I liked it better long."

"And I like it better short." She took a small sip

of wine. "Cam didn't know you were in San Francisco."

"He does now. I contacted him this morning and he's sharing my suite at the Fairmont." Jordan took her glass and set it on the table beside them. "Let's get out of here. I need to talk to you."

Sara felt a swift surge of panic. "I don't want to leave. I just got here. I haven't even said hello to Mac."

"For God's sake, Sara, stop—" He broke off and she could see him struggling with his exasperation. "Very well, we'll stay. Where can we find some privacy in this crowd?"

"We don't need privacy. We have nothing to say to each other."

"The hell we don't." His glance quickly raked the room and then he grabbed her arm and began propelling her through the crowd to the French doors leading to the terrace. "We need to have a conversation that's long overdue." He opened a door and gestured for her to precede him. "And one you cheated me out of when you ran away from Half Moon."

"I didn't run away. I left a note explaining why—" She heard the sudden harsh intake of his breath and glanced back over her shoulder at him. His gaze was fastened on the gleaming expanse of silken flesh revealed by the deep V of her gown.

"Dammit, why did you ever bother to put that rag on? You might as well have come here naked."

She stiffened. "It's in good taste. If you had your way, I'd always be bundled up to my eyebrows. You wouldn't even let me wear shorts out-side the house!"

He scowled. "You looked too sexy." He followed her out on the deserted terrace and closed the door. "And I thought it was a joint decision. We agreed—"

"Agreed?" She whirled to face him. "We never agreed on anything. You decided and then set about getting me to do exactly what you wanted."

"And you enjoyed every minute of it."

Her face felt suddenly hot. "You're an expert lover, Jordan. You know how to push every one of my buttons. During those months with you I felt as if I were wandering around in some kind of erotic dream." She met his gaze. "But there al-ways comes a time to wake up to reality, and when I did, I realized what you'd done to me—"

"It *was* real." Jordan's voice was charged with soft violence. "We were real. You loved every single thing we did together." He took a step closer. "You're the most responsive woman I've ever met. Do you remember how many times a day we made love? How the tears would run down your cheeks and you'd dig your nails into my shoulders? Do you remember that, Sara?"

She took a step back and tried to close her mind against him. She would *not* remember those moments of sexual insanity. "I remember that you persuaded me to give up my career. I remem-ber that you discouraged every friendship I tried to make. I remember that before I managed to break free from you I was on the way to being sexually subjugated."

A flicker of pain darkened his face. "You make me sound like something out of de Sade. I was never cruel to you, Sara, and I always tried to give you everything you could want."

"Did you ever ask me what I wanted?" She smiled sadly. "And no, you were never physically cruel to me."

His lips twisted. "I suppose the implication is that I raped you mentally?"

"That's as good a word as any. You most certainly manipulated me. You're very good at manipulating people. I believe sometimes you aren't even aware that you're doing it. Well, I'm through being manipulated by anyone." She turned toward the French doors. "I gave Cam my answer last night. I'm not coming back to you, Jordan. Find another mindless woman to play your bed games with."

"They weren't games. Lord, I thought you knew that."

Sara refused to look back at him as she crossed the terrace. She could feel his gaze on her naked back and a hot shiver ran through her. Her body had once been so sensually attuned to him that he had only to look at her for her breasts to swell and the hunger to begin to stir between her thighs. It was happening again now, she realized and acute anxiety welled up in her. Just another minute and she'd be back in the apartment and could lose herself in the crowd. Just another minute.

"I'm not letting you go."

"You don't have any choice." She opened the door. "Good-bye, Jordan."

Jordan's hands slowly closed into fists at his sides. He could see the pale gleam of her hair through the sheer panels that curtained the French doors and then she was lost to view. He had made a complete botch of it, he thought with profound self-disgust. He had planned on being gentle and understanding, of telling her he realized what an idiot he had been. Instead, he had argued and defended himself and, as the pièce de résistance, had actually stated his claim on her. After this fiasco he'd be lucky if she didn't go to the police and get a restraining order to keep him from bothering her.

He should have known he would blow it. He had only to be in the same room with Sara to respond with instinctive possessiveness. He'd hoped their time apart would have tempered his reaction, and heaven knew he had been battling his nature for the last eighteen months.

It was clearly still too soon. His body wanted her too much and old habits were hard to break. He should have forced himself to wait until he was sure he could act with discipline and restraint. But circumstances had placed him in a position in which he could no longer wait. A cold chill had touched him when Cam had told him about the deserted warehouse where Sara now lived; there was no way he could let her go her own way while she lived in such a dangerous place and that madman from New York still on the loose.

That memory suddenly brought another possibility to mind. Sara had been very upset when she had left him just seconds ago. He had learned to read every nuance of her responses and recognized that her control was barely skin deep. What if she had left the party to drive alone back to that damned warehouse on the docks? Hell, she might have left already.

He muttered a curse beneath his breath as he strode swiftly across the terrace and jerked open a French door, his gaze anxiously searching the crowd.

Two

The dark blue Mercedes pulled into the warehouse directly behind Sara's Honda, its tires screeching on the tarmac.

Sara's heart jerked with fear. Then, as she saw Jordan step from behind the wheel, it jerked again with an entirely different apprehension. She had hoped it was over. She *wanted* it to be over, dammit.

She got out of her car and slammed the door shut. "This is private property, Jordan. That means you have to be invited on the premises."

"It's too private. I couldn't believe it when Cam told me about the setup here. Don't you have any sense? This is a perfect place for an attack. Talk about invitations."

"This is a very well-patrolled neighborhood," she said defensively. "And it's none of your business anyway. Go away, Jordan."

"When you're safely in your apartment."

"No, I don't—" But he was already striding toward the elevator and she found herself hurrying after him. "I don't need to have an escort to my front door. I've gotten along quite well without you for some time."

"Sure you have." He turned to face her, his expression grim under the illumination of the bulb over the elevator. "You position yourself so that you're number one on a serial killer's hit list and then move into a deserted warehouse on the waterfront. Why don't you go back to New York and hand him a knife to cut your throat?"

She gazed at him in bewilderment. "How did you know about Kemp?"

Jordan didn't answer.

"How, Jordan?"

"It was in all the newspapers," he said evasively.

"I doubt if the Australian papers would have carried it. That's not how you knew, is it?" She studied him intently. "Were you in Sausalito yesterday?"

The slightest flicker of expression crossed his face.

"You were following me," she whispered. "How long?"

"I've been here for only three weeks."

"Three weeks? Cam didn't even know you'd left Half Moon." She suddenly remembered Cam's odd expression when she had questioned him about Jordan's whereabouts. "Or maybe he did know. Was he lying to me?"

Jordan was silent a moment and then slowly shook his head. "You should know better than that. Cam doesn't lie." His smile was bittersweet. "He has all the scruples in the family, remember?"

"But there was something he wasn't telling me?"

"Is this how you conduct your interviews for *World Report*?" He shrugged. "Cam probably suspected I was here. He knew I'd been here several times in the last year."

"Several times . . ." She shook her head dazedly. "Why, for heaven's sake?"

"I wanted to be near you," he said simply.

She felt as if the breath had been knocked out of her. Her initial anger was beginning to melt away, but she tried desperately to hold on to it. "So you *followed* me? What right did you have to do that?"

"I wanted to keep you safe. Kemp—"

"It sounds *obsessive.*"

"I didn't trail after you like a hungry wolf. I do have my own work, too, you know. I hired an agency to make sure you were safe when I couldn't be on the spot."

"Detectives? You hired detectives to follow me?" She shook her head in wonder. "You always did keep an eagle eye on your possessions." She fumbled desperately in her purse for her key ring. "But this is the one who got away."

Jordan flinched. "I never regarded you as only a possession, Sara."

"Really? You could have fooled me." She laughed shakily as she unlocked the elevator and pushed back the gate. "How did you regard me?"

"As my love."

She closed her eyes. "Don't do this to me, Jordan. Don't lie to me."

"I'm not lying," he said huskily. "Come back to me and let me show you how good it can be for us."

She whirled to face him, her lids opening to reveal eyes blazing with anger and desperation. "How can I trust you? I *know* you, Jordan. You can't bear to give up anything that belongs to you. You'd do anything to get your own way."

"You're right, I'd do anything to get you to come back to me." He paused. "Anything."

Everything he said was like raw acid on an open wound. "It's no good. We had nothing on which to build a relationship."

"You didn't give us a chance," he said hoarsely. "You could have talked to me, told me how you felt. You didn't have to run away from me."

"Every time I tried to talk to you we ended up in bed. We wanted different things from our marriage. It would never have worked out." She stepped into the elevator. "Good night, Jordan."

He was right behind her. "I'm coming with you." Then, as she started to protest, he said roughly, "Don't worry, I'll leave you pristine pure at your front door. I just want to make sure no one is waiting upstairs." He closed the gate and pressed the button. The elevator started with its characteristic lurch and then began its snail's-pace ascent.

"How could someone get upstairs to wait for me since the elevator is locked?"

"There are such things as master keys."

He was too close. He wasn't touching her but she could still feel the heat emanating from his body and smell the clean fragrance of soap and that lemony aftershave that was as familiar to her as her own favorite perfume. Why did the blasted elevator have to move so slowly?

She could feel his gaze on her face and knew he was aware of the quickening tempo of the pulse in her temple. He had always been aware of the slightest betrayal in her responses and used that knowledge to launch his assaults with devastating effectiveness.

"Do you remember the first time you rode in the private elevator at my office in Sydney?"

She stiffened and felt the muscles of her abdomen tense as an explosion of heat tore through her. "No."

"I do." His voice was velvet soft in her ear. "We'd been married only a few weeks and you decided you wanted to visit Bandor Tower and see where I worked. We'd just made love that morning but it hadn't been enough for either of us. Something exploded between us. I stopped the elevator between the floors . . ."

Sara felt her breasts tauten and swell beneath the soft velvet of the bodice of her gown as the memory of those wild and primitive moments in the elevator replayed in her mind: Jordan's frantic urgency as he had pulled her down on the carpeted floor of the elevator, his face strained with hunger above her, her own cries as he had driven into her again and again and again. . . .

He took a half step back in the elevator, and she could feel his gaze on her naked flesh as she had on the terrace. "Lord, you have beautiful skin." His index finger touched her with whisper lightness in the exact hollow of her spine. "Pale and satin smooth."

His finger moved slowly up her spine to her shoulder blades, leaving a trail of fire and aching pleasure in its wake.

The elevator had stopped. She should open the gate, she thought desperately, but she couldn't seem to move. She was rooted, bound by the gossamer pressure of Jordan's finger on her flesh, captured by the pleasure he was giving her. His finger moved down again, tracing the line of her spine past her waist to the point where her gown ended and her buttocks began to swell gently against the velvet. "And your bottom is absolutely magnificent." She could hear the harshness of his breathing behind her, and its roughness stroked her, readied her with the same power as the gentleness of his finger. "I have only to watch you walk across the room to get turned on. Not that you wriggle, you just have a little swing that's full of joy and freedom. I could never get enough of watching you move, Sara." His hands suddenly slipped beneath the velvet of the gown to cup her buttocks in his palms.

She gasped, her spine arching as she felt a tingle of hunger that was like an electric shock.

"It's been so *long*." Jordan's low voice held a note of torment. His hands squeezed gently, rhythmically. "Sometimes I thought I'd go crazy if I couldn't come inside you and feel you moving."

Her eyes closed as she half-leaned back against his shoulder. She wanted to part her legs and feel Jordan's hands slide around to cup, tease, satisfy. All she had to do was to make the move and Jordan would give her what she needed. Jordan always knew how to please her. He seemed to read her mind when it came to physical pleasure. It was the only time she felt close to him.

Because that physical nearness was the only part of him that he would share with her.

The thought brought a rush of pain that chilled the heat of the desire Jordan was building so skillfully. "No!" She pulled away and he slid his hands quickly up her back. She fumbled at the gate until she finally managed to get it open. Then she was across the corridor unlocking the door to her loft. "No way!"

"Sara . . ." Jordan was beside her, his voice urgent in her ear. "Let me come in. You know you want it. You know you want *me*."

She turned to face him, her eyes blazing in her pale face. "Yes, I want you. But it doesn't matter. Do you understand? I want a husband who can give me more than you're offering me. I want to know what my husband is thinking, what he's feeling. I want to be so close to him that there's a oneness, a sweetness, a kind of—" She could feel the tears stinging behind her eyes and was forced to stop. "Oh, what's the use? You probably don't even know what I mean."

"I know." Jordan's voice was halting. "But I'm not sure I can give you what you want."

"Well, when I left Half Moon I swore I'd never settle for anything less again." She turned away. "So perhaps you'd better just forget about me."

"I can't forget," he said harshly. "How can I make you see that I'll never be able to forget you?"

"You can't, dammit." Sara stepped into the apartment and slammed the door.

She wilted against the mahogany panels, feeling suddenly weak. She had come so close to giving in to him. She was still trembling in the aftermath of the desire and emotion he had aroused. But she had faced him and hadn't succumbed, she told herself. Next time it would be easier. Dear sweet heaven, she *hoped* it would be easier.

Jordan turned away and stepped back into the elevator. A muscle in his left cheek jerked as he put the elevator in motion. Two minutes later he was in the driver's seat of the Mercedes, gazing blindly into the darkness. The pain would lessen soon and then he'd be able to think again. All he had to do was to hold on until— He leaned forward and rested his forehead on the steering wheel, his hands clasping it with white-knuckled force.

Several minutes later he lifted his head and forced his grip to loosen on the steering wheel. His control was reasserting itself. Now he would sit here and think about what Sara had said and try to make plans. Heaven only knew that he had plenty of time to do it. He had told Marambas he wouldn't be needed tonight and there was no way he was going to leave Sara unguarded.

The ruby and diamond bracelet was delivered to Sara the next morning at the office of *World Report* by messenger. The black velvet jeweler's box contained no card.

At two in the afternoon a full-length Russian sable coat arrived together with a box of long-stemmed yellow roses. No card was enclosed.

At four o'clock the manager of the parking lot downstairs phoned her to say that the keys to her Lamborghini had been delivered to him for safe-keeping. Did she wish him to send them up?

"No." Her hand tightened on the receiver. "Was there a note with the keys?"

The answer was the one she had expected. No note. She slowly hung up the receiver and gazed numbly at the cream-colored phone on the desk.

"Jordan?" Penny asked.

"I guess it has to be. Who else would send a hundred-thousand-dollar car without a note?" Sara shook her head in bewilderment. "Why is he doing this?"

"You'd know that better than I." Penny made a face. "But you'd better make sure it stops. You know how Mac feels about personal matters intruding at the office."

"It will stop. I'll make sure it stops, and damn quick." Sara slipped the jeweler's box into her purse and draped the sable over one arm. "I'll see you tomorrow, Penny."

"You don't have to see him again. You could use a messenger service."

"Rubies, sables, and a Lamborghini?" Sara shook her head. "Would you risk any one of those to a messenger service?"

"Jordan did." A glint of respect gleamed in Penny's brown eyes. "He's not stupid. If he intended to force you to see him again, he certainly chose a unique way to do it."

"Oh, yes, Jordan is nothing if not unique." Sara whirled and strode out of the newsroom.

Forty-five minutes later she was standing in front of Jordan's door at the Fairmont, pounding briskly on it.

"Why?" she asked as soon as Jordan threw open the door. She marched into the suite, handed him the jewelry box, and threw the sable coat and the car keys on the white suede couch. "You knew I wouldn't take them."

"You were pretty upset last night and I was afraid you wouldn't see me again." Jordan closed the door and leaned back against it. "I thought this would be a way to kill the proverbial two birds with one stone."

"Two?"

He nodded. "Getting you to see me and beginning our courtship."

She gazed at him in disbelief. "Courtship? We're getting a divorce."

He shook his head. "Not in the next hundred years, love. You'll be a little gray-haired lady in a wheelchair before you untie the legal knots my lawyers are busy thinking up."

"Jordan, be reasonable. I'm not going to change my mind."

"You will." His lips tightened. "And I would have thought you'd realize that I'm never reasonable about anything concerning you." He straightened away from the door. "I'm trying to give you what you want from me. You said you'd never gotten to know me. Well, you're going to know me better than you do your best friend before we're done. I thought about it for a long time last night and I decided what you needed was a courtship." He smiled faintly. "If you remember, we ended up in bed together the second time we met and were married by the end of the week. That didn't give us much time for the conventional rituals."

"Jordan . . ." She gazed at him in despair. "It's too late. This isn't going to work."

"It *will* work." Jordan's voice vibrated with intensity. "You think I have some kinky sexual obsession for your very lovely body. Well, maybe I do find making love to you addictive, but that doesn't mean that's all there is to it. I *love* you, dammit."

She felt the faintest stirring of hope. "I can't believe you."

He took an impulsive step toward her and then stopped as she took a swift step backward. "Sorry, it's an automatic reflex to try to hold you." His voice was suddenly fierce. "But that doesn't mean it's wrong. What we have together sexually is damn beautiful." He drew a deep breath. "So the courtship begins. Shall I tell you how we're going to conduct it?"

She nodded slowly.

"No sex."

Her eyes widened in surprise.

"I'm shocked as hell myself." His lips curved in a smile. "I assure you, if I could accomplish what I need to do without that particular abstention, I'd move heaven and earth to do it. But sex seems to be the crux of the entire problem. You think that's all I want from you and that it's the weapon I use to manipulate you. Right?"

She nodded again.

"So I don't touch you and I don't manipulate you. We date, we talk, we court. Okay?"

"What if I say no, that it's not okay?"

The faintest flicker of humor showed on his face. "Then you'll receive a present at *World Report* every hour on the hour. I'll follow you around like a lonesome puppy"—and his voice lowered to velvet softness— "I'll try to seduce you at every opportunity."

"I see." Her gaze searched his face. "This isn't a trick? You really mean it?"

He flinched. "My God, I don't break my word, Sara."

"I realize your promise is respected among your business associates, but I don't really know . . ."

"You will before our courtship is over. Well?"

It would probably be a terrible mistake, Sara thought. Jordan was an enigma. He had told her he would do anything to get her back, and perhaps this was just another ploy to disarm her. She started to tell him she wouldn't do it.

"Please," he muttered.

She felt a melting deep within her. Jordan had always demanded, taken, or seduced. She couldn't remember him ever pleading for anything in their entire time together. Could there still be hope? Oh, Lord, did she want there to be hope? Her life was so serene now with no Jordan to stir and bewitch her senses.

"Trust me. I'll never try to manipulate you again."

Trust him. There had never been trust between them, only passion and physical delight. Yet, if he sincerely meant what he said, the prospect for a deeper happiness would then be beyond anything she had dreamed.

"Sara, answer me."

"I'll trust you. For now," she said slowly, then paused. "But if you're going to court me, it's damn well going to be a normal, everyday courtship. Call off those private investigators and stop following me around yourself."

Relief flickered across his face and the tension eased from his taut muscles. "Right. You won't be sorry."

She met his gaze. "If I am, it will be the last time," she said deliberately. "I won't go through this again. I'm not a masochist, Jordan."

"No threats." He smiled and looked suddenly boyish. "It's going to be all right, Sara. Just relax and let me do the worrying."

She sighed. "There you go again. I like doing my

share of the worrying. It indicates a relationship and not a form of thralldom."

"Sorry." His bright blue eyes twinkled. "It's—"

"Automatic," she finished for him. She found herself smiling. "You have a long way to go."

"But I'll get there." His smile vanished. "With a little help from you. I've never asked you for help before, Sara. Help me to make this work."

The silence between them was suddenly fraught with emotion, and Sara found herself staring up at him, unable to tear her gaze away. He was asking something from her beyond what the words expressed. Something deeper. She finally managed to look away and laugh shakily. "Well, I need some help too. Mac's going to raise the roof if you continue to send gifts to the office. It doesn't strike quite the right note of professionalism in the newsroom. No more presents. Okay?"

"No more presents." He glanced wistfully at the sable coat she had tossed on the couch when she entered the apartment. "I don't suppose you'd be willing to accept these—"

"No," she said firmly.

"Pity. Oh, well, I'll save them until you decide—" He broke off and gave her a sheepish smile as he saw the wariness dawning in her face. "I know. You don't have to tell me. I'm pushing. I'm afraid it's the nature of the beast."

"I noticed," she said dryly. "For nine solid months."

"It will be different this time. I promise you, Sara." He suddenly turned away and opened the door. "I'll pick you up at seven. Be ready. There's something I want to show you."

She was obviously being dismissed, Sara thought with amusement. "It's customary to request the pleasure of the lady's company," she said lightly. "In fact, it's considered *de rigueur* during court-ship, Jordan."

He smiled. "Will you please come with me to-night?"

"I'd be delighted." Sara turned at the door to look up at him. "What do I wear? Formal or informal?"

"Jeans, tennis shoes, and a Windbreaker. See you at seven."

She could feel his gaze on her as she walked down the hall toward the elevators. What had she gotten herself into? she wondered apprehensively. It was beginning again; she was being swayed by Jordan as if she had never left him.

She stopped short as she reached the elevators and glanced over her shoulder. Jordan was still standing in the doorway watching her as if he'd known she'd have second thoughts. He probably had known, damn him.

Then he smiled with such loving understanding, she felt her anxiety ebbing away. "It's all right, love," he called softly. "You're not making a mistake." He slowly shut the door.

For some odd reason she was reassured. She pushed the button for the elevator. After all, she was doing nothing irrevocable, surely there was no harm in giving Jordan his chance to prove her wrong about him.

Where could he be taking her this evening? She would have expected candlelight and seductive soft music for Jordan to initiate his courtship. Not jeans and tennis shoes.

Sara gazed in bewilderment at the massive steel skeleton of the skyscraper towering against the sunset sky. "*This* is what you wanted me to see?"

Jordan nodded as he handed her a bright yellow hardhat. "Put this on. I want to take you up on the top girders. There's a great view of the bay." He put on his own hat and took her hand to help her down the dirt incline from the street. "It will be another four months before it's finished, but you can see how it's going to shape up."

"Is it a new hotel?"

Jordan shook his head. "It's the new headquarters for Bandor International. I'm moving the entire executive structure from Sydney to San Francisco."

Her eyes widened in surprise. "Why?"

"You like it here." Jordan didn't look at her as he helped her over the rough ground, carefully avoiding bulldozers and power tools. "And I think you'll feel safer on your home ground." His hand tightened around her own. "I want you to feel secure with me. Maybe you would have felt more capable of trying to work things out if you hadn't been forced to live in a strange country."

"You're moving because of me?" she whispered. "What if it doesn't suc—"

"I told you our marriage is going to work this time." He pulled her into the outside construction elevator and turned the switch. The elevator moved swiftly upward. "By the way, this is how a lift is supposed to work. Why don't you let me send a team of workmen to your building to replace that antique?"

"I like that elevator. It has character."

A sudden smile warmed his face. "I remember you said the old beat-up Volkswagen you owned in Sydney had character."

She stiffened. He had opened an old wound. "I *liked* it. You had no right to get rid of it and buy me another one."

"Dammit, I was worried about that old clunker breaking down in traffic," he said, clearly exasperated. "I had nightmares about you ending up in the hospital or the morgue."

"You did?" She was startled. "Why didn't you tell me you were worried? I'm not unreasonable. I just thought you didn't want your wife driving a car that looked like it was ready for the junk heap."

"I thought you'd realize I . . ." He trailed off, gazing straight ahead. "I'm an inarticulate bastard when it comes to talking about things that are important to me. It's as if it's all locked up inside me and can't get out." The elevator had come to a stop and he stepped out onto the girder. "Be careful. The girders are laid pretty close together here and there's a safety railing." His hold on her arm was painfully tight as he drew her carefully over to the edge of the structure. "Sit down."

She plopped down, dangling her legs over the edge of the building. She breathed in the air's piercing coolness, her gaze on the blue-violet bay in the distance. "You're right, it's a beautiful view. I'm glad you brought me to see it. It gives you a strange feeling being up here, doesn't it?"

"What do you mean?" He sat down beside her. His hand once more closing tightly on her arm. "Scoot back a little. You're too close to the edge."

Sara moved back a few inches. "I don't know. I guess it gives me a sense of my fragility to look at those massive concrete skyscrapers and realize that all of it started just like this. Girders and wires and space . . ." She gestured helplessly. "Do you know what I'm trying to say?"

"That they're all raw and unfinished beneath the facade." The expression on his face was amazingly gentle as he gazed at her. "And so are we all."

She nodded. "Yes, but there's something else there too. There has to be strength and endurance or there wouldn't be anything to build on. We'd just crumble away."

"Not you. You're a very strong lady."

"You think I'm strong?" She gazed at him in surprise. "I didn't show much strength when I was with you or I wouldn't have let you dominate me as you did."

"I always knew you were strong." He looked out over the city. "It scared the hell out of me."

"Scared you? You're joking."

He shook his head. "It's easy to control the weak, but it's nearly impossible to control the strong. I knew if I wasn't very clever I'd never be able to control you." He turned and met her gaze. "And I *was* clever. I studied you and concentrated every particle of my energy on finding the ways to do so."

She gazed at him, stunned. "Why?"

"I didn't want to lose you." He smiled crookedly. "And then I lost you anyway. Which proves I'm not such a clever fellow after all, doesn't it?"

"Why are you telling me this?"

"For the same reason I tried to control you. Everything I do is based on that same basic theme. If I'm not honest with you, I may lose you." He pointed across the bay. "I've bought some property outside of Sausalito. When you're ready to choose the architect for our house, I'll take you to look at it."

She shook her head. "Office buildings, houses. You're moving too fast."

"I've had eighteen months of waiting, so my actions now seem damn slow to me." Jordan rose to his feet. "We'd better go down. It isn't safe on these girders after dark." He pulled her up beside him and his grip was viselike as he helped her across the roof to the elevator. A moment later they were descending to the ground.

She suddenly became aware that Jordan's hand

on the switch was trembling. Her gaze lifted swiftly to his face to find it pale and strained. "Jordan, what's wrong?"

He smiled. "It's nothing. It just scared me to see you skipping along those girders."

"Then why did you take me up there?"

The elevator came to a halt and he stepped out and took her elbow. "A little test."

"For me?"

"No, for me. Eighteen months ago I wouldn't have been able to stand to see you up there." He began to propel her across the construction site. "But I made it and that's saying something, I guess."

"I don't understand."

They had reached the sidewalk and he stopped and turned her to face him. He took off her yellow hardhat, his fingers lingering on the sleek softness of her hair. "It's not enough for you to get to know me. I have to get to know myself. I have to learn what's possible for me and what's going to be impossible."

She gazed at him in puzzlement. The last rays of twilight lent an odd sternness to the hard planes contouring his face. "Perhaps we both have some learning to do," she said slowly. "I seem to be finding out new things about you every moment now."

He grimaced. "I'm surprised I haven't sent you flying for sanctuary. Honesty may be the best policy, but it's not always the safest."

"No, it's not." A smile lit her face. "But I believe I like you better with a few holes in your armor."

He chuckled. "You mean like that disaster of a Volkswagen and that godawful lift?"

"Character is very important," she assured him gravely. "And rough edges are always more interesting than smooth ones."

He took off his own yellow hardhat and started toward the Mercedes parked down the street. "Come on, I'll take you to a coffee shop and let you see if you can discover a few more of my hard edges. Lord knows, I have enough of them."

"I really should go home. I have to work tomorrow."

He turned and his eyes narrowed as he studied her intently. "Your work is very important to you, isn't it? I've read several of your interviews in the past months and found them quite perceptive."

"Thank you. I enjoy doing interviews more than conventional articles. It's a challenge to be able to dig deep and find out what motivates and drives the people who have an effect on all of us." She made a face. "Unfortunately, most of those people don't need publicity and I have the devil of a time arranging interviews. For instance, I'd give my eye teeth for a chance at an interview with Alex Ben Raschid or Margaret Thatcher, but I haven't had any luck as yet."

"For a woman of your determination I'm sure it's only a question of time." He smiled faintly. "No coffee, then?"

She hesitated.

"If I try to persuade you to go, you're sure to

accuse me of trying to manipulate you. So it's your decision, Sara."

Her decision, not Jordan's. She felt a sudden explosion of exuberance that almost made her dizzy. "It is, isn't it?" She jammed her hands in the pockets of her Windbreaker and strolled after him. "And I don't feel like going home right now."

He lifted one dark brow, waiting.

"And I do feel like going to a coffeehouse."

He inclined his head in a mocking bow. "I'm truly honored, milady." He opened the door of the Mercedes. "I'll make every attempt to get you home before the witching hour."

"How did it go?" Cam asked as soon as Jordan walked into the suite a few minutes after midnight. "Success?"

Jordan shook his head. "Hope." He crossed to the telephone on the desk and lifted the receiver. "I figure that's success enough for the moment."

"My, how humble we're becoming." Cam's eyes were twinkling. "Is this the real Jordan Bandor speaking?"

"Get off my back, brat." Jordan quickly punched in a number. "I have enough pressure at the moment without you needling me. I promised Sara I'd call off the detectives."

Cam gave a low whistle. "And you're going to do it?"

"I gave her my word." Jordan's grip tightened on the receiver. "And I'll keep it. I'll just have to find a way to keep her safe without surrounding her with bodyguards."

"And how will you do that?"

"Spend as much time with her as possible." He smiled lopsidedly. "I'd do that anyway." The phone started to ring at the other end of the line. "And, if I can't keep a guard on her, I'll do the next best thing. I'll set Marambas's people to watching Kemp in New York. With the police and Marambas's men both on surveillance, there shouldn't be any possibility Kemp will slip away from them." The phone was picked up and Marambas answered. Jordan spoke into the receiver. "Marambas, there's been a change of plan. Here's what I want you to do."

Two minutes later he replaced the receiver and stood looking down at the phone with a thoughtful frown.

"Mission accomplished?" Cam asked.

"What?" Jordan's tone was abstracted. "Oh, yes, he said he'd get on it right away." He reached for the receiver again. "It's still a decent hour in Sedikhan, isn't it?"

"Sedikhan?" Cam looked at him in surprise. "I think so. I get turned around after I've been in a place for more than a few days. Why are you calling Sedikhan?"

Jordan didn't answer. He was already speaking to the international operator.

Three

"You look tired. Rough flight?"

Sara's heart gave a sudden leap as she turned and saw Jordan leaning against the wall beside the door exiting airport customs. He was casually dressed in worn jeans and the sleeves of his cream-colored shirt were rolled up to the elbow. His arms were crossed over his chest and he looked calm, strong, and wonderfully unfrazzled in the hubbub surrounding her. "No more than usual, but Sedik-han is a heck of a long way. I suppose I've got jet lag. It was nice of you to come to meet me. I didn't expect anyone to show up in the middle of the night." Her gaze narrowed on his face. "I don't suppose you'd like to tell me how you knew what flight I'd be on? What is there between you and Mac Devlin anyway? You two looked like bosom buddies at his party."

"I scarcely know Mac. We do have a few business affiliations." He picked up her garment bag and overnight case. "It wasn't he who told me when you'd be coming in. My car is in the parking lot. Can you manage that attaché case?"

She nodded as she fell into step with him. "How *did* you know? The trip was so hurried, I didn't have time to make return reservations before I reached Sedikhan."

He smiled faintly. "No detectives, I promise."

"Jordan, dammit, tell me—" She stopped, her eyes widening. "Wait just a minute . . . You wouldn't, by any chance, also be a bosom buddy of Alex Ben Raschid's?"

"Alex and I are acquainted. Bandor Enterprises recently built a hotel in Marasef and I spent a few weekends at the palace when I was in Sedikhan seven months ago. Alex is a very interesting man. How did your interview with him turn out?"

"Wonderfully. It may be the best thing I've ever done. He projects so much color and force." She stopped by the passenger door of the Mercedes and turned to face him. "You did it, didn't you? I thought it was weird that the sheikh's secretary would suddenly call Mac to set up an interview, when he'd been refusing to see me for over a year. You pulled strings to get me that interview."

"Alex wouldn't have given you an interview if you hadn't had a solid reputation in your field." Jordan unlocked the door and put the luggage in the backseat. "When he phoned to tell me the deed was done, he said he was very impressed with you so you probably would have gotten the interview eventually anyway. I merely accelerated the process."

She reached out impulsively to grasp his arm. "But why did you do it?"

He tensed and his gaze fell to her hand on his arm. Her gaze followed his own and she was suddenly acutely conscious of the pale slenderness of her fingers against the bronze muscularity of his forearm . . . of the warmth of his skin . . . of the magnetic vitality he exuded as an almost palpable force.

She quickly withdrew her hand and smiled with an effort. "I thought we'd agreed there'd be no more presents."

"This wasn't a present. It was reparation."

"Reparation?"

He nodded. "I took nine months out of your career when I persuaded you to give it up when we were married. Since I stole something you valued, it was only right that I give you something you valued in return."

She swallowed to ease the sudden tightness in her throat. "Alex Ben Raschid on a silver platter?"

His rare warm smile lightened the gravity of his face. "I doubt if anyone would dare even to try to serve Alex up on any kind of dish, but I'm glad if I could help. I'm afraid you'll have to get Margaret Thatcher on your own. I've never met the lady." He helped her into the car and in another moment was sliding into the driver's seat beside her.

"Lean back and relax. If you go to sleep, I'll wake you when I get you home."

She shook her head. "Drop me off at *World Report.* I have to file my story right away or it won't get in this week's issue."

"It's after three o'clock in the morning. You're exhausted." The sudden violence in his voice startled her. "Why the hell can't it wait until—" He stopped as he saw her expression, and when he spoke again his tone was totally controlled. "You absolutely must file it tonight?"

She nodded. "Deadlines. It goes with the territory."

"Okay." He backed the Mercedes out of the parking space. "I'll drive you to your office and wait outside until you've finished your work. Then I'll drive you home."

She frowned. "That's crazy. It may be hours before I'm free to leave. Just drop me off and I'll take a taxi back to the loft."

"I'll wait for you," he repeated. He met her gaze and smiled faintly. "As you said, it goes with the territory."

The knock on the door was loud and authoritative.

"I'll be right there." Sara snatched up her Windbreaker lying on the bed and hurried toward the door. "You're early." She threw open the door. "I expected—"

"But the unexpected is always more interesting." Cam grinned as he leaned forward to plant a kiss on the tip of her nose. "You should have learned that by now, Sara. Jordan seldom does what anyone expects him to do."

"I thought you'd gone back to Papeete. Jordan didn't mention you were still here." She gave him a quick hug, feeling the warm affection that Cam always managed to instill in everyone he met. "Why didn't you call me?"

"According to Jordan, he's been keeping you pretty busy himself for the last week or so. I thought I'd keep a low profile until you and Jordan had a chance to work things out." His smile faded. "Lord, I'm glad that's happening, luv."

"So am I," she said softly. "But it's too early yet to do anything but hope."

"You sound like Jordan." His gaze searched her face. "Hope seems to be enough to make you light up inside, though."

Sara wasn't surprised she was giving that impression. She sometimes thought the radiance blossoming inside her could light up all of San Francisco. "You were right about Jordan. He has changed." She had never dreamed Jordan could be as gentle and restrained as he had been this last week. He had shown her an entirely different side of his nature. She had always known he was brilliant and charismatic, but she had never realized he could be both understanding and kind.

"I'm glad to hear it." Cam's dark eyes were gentle. "Have you finally got yourself a friend in him?"

"Not yet. But maybe I will soon, Cam." She felt a

rush of wild joy. Very soon. She could feel it coming, sense it just beyond the horizon. She slipped into her jacket. "Jordan is supposed to be here any minute to take me to see a building site he bought across the bay. Why don't you come with us?"

"The plans are changed. Jordan called and asked me to pick you up. He gave me directions and said he'd meet us there."

Sara experienced a slight uneasiness mixed with disappointment. "Oh, I guess he was too busy to come himself." It wasn't reasonable of her to expect to receive Jordan's undivided attention. After all, he'd spent nearly every evening with her since the night she'd returned from Sedikhan. Yet she *was* disappointed, dammit.

Cam shrugged. "Search me. He said something about a test. I don't know what the hell he was talking about."

"I think I do," she said softly, remembering Jordan's words of the evening they had sat on the girders overlooking the city. He was challenging himself again, fighting his possessiveness and jealousy as he had his fear for her. "I believe I know exactly what he meant." She linked her arm with Cam's as she shut the door behind her. "Come along, Cam, I have a hunch this is going to be a splendiferous afternoon."

He frowned, puzzled. "If you say so. Personally, I'm not wild about trekking all over the countryside. I'm strictly a city boy." He added hastily,

"But if I'm forced to endure all this bucolic nonsense, I'm glad it's with such pleasant company."

"Knock it off, Cam," she said as they entered the elevator. "I'm only your sister-in-law. Save your gallantry for more important prey."

"I'm always gallant," he said indignantly. "It's part of my irresistible charm."

The afternoon was just as wonderful as Sara had hoped it would be. She could feel the happiness bubbling inside her as she paced the building site, chatting gaily with Cam and Jordan. She couldn't seem to keep still. The sunlight was too golden, the sky too blue, her mood too ebullient to hide what she was feeling. She ran back and forth like an eager puppy, pointing out the view of the bay and then the beautiful stand of eucalyptus that bordered the northern boundary of the property. "There's nothing that smells better than eucalyptus. Do you remember that huge ghost gum tree at Half Moon? I used to breathe in the scent and think there was absolutely nothing—" She broke off as she intercepted the indulgent smiles Cam and Jordan were exchanging. She made a face at both of them. "Have I ever told you how I hate to be patronized?" She whirled in a circle. "But I refuse to let either of you macho Australian types bother me. I feel too *good*."

Jordan shook his head, his hard mouth curving in a smile that was strangely gentle. "Perhaps we're not being patronizing so much as envious.

It's been a long time since I've been able to get that much joy out of life. It's . . . rather wonderful."

She stood laughing at him, lifting her hand to brush away a tousled lock of fair hair from her face. He was the one who was wonderful, she thought. Sunlight glinted on his dark hair and the strong breeze flattened his blue chambray shirt against his broad chest and whipped color into his face, warming the bronze of his skin. He was standing with his legs parted, his worn jeans outlining his slim hips and muscular thighs with loving detail. He looked totally male and so sensual she could feel a tingle of heat go through her as she looked at him. It came as a shock. Jordan had kept all hint of sexuality from his demeanor for the last week and made no attempt to arouse her in any way. He wasn't trying now, but that didn't prevent her from responding to the animal magnetism that was one of his most salient characteristics. She found her laughter dying as her breath caught in her throat.

He knew what she was feeling. She could see it in the sudden stillness of his face. She moistened her lips nervously with her tongue and felt her nipples hardening against the cotton of her T-shirt. She should look away. It was far too soon to risk a sexual encounter with Jordan. If her mind knew that, why couldn't her body be equally sensible? It was readying itself, the heat cascading through her. Yes, she should definitely look away.

It was Jordan who looked away. He turned and glanced out over the bay. "We'd better start back."

His words were clipped, the lines of his body taut. "You drive her home, Cam." He started across the grass to the Mercedes parked on the road.

Happiness. Wild, shining happiness. He had known how vulnerable she was in that moment and had made no move to take advantage of her weakness. No manipulation, no seduction, just honesty, restraint, integrity. "Wait." Her voice was lilting. "Wait, Jordan."

He stopped but didn't turn around. She was conscious of the tension that corded his every muscle. "Yes?"

"I want to throw a party. You've never met my friends here and I'd like you to get to know some of them. Why don't you and Cam come tonight and we'll open a few bottles of wine and—"

"Not tonight."

"You're busy?" She couldn't keep the disappointment from her voice. "I know it's short notice but—"

He muttered something beneath his breath. "Very well, I'll be there." Then he was again striding toward the Mercedes.

"I didn't mean I wanted him to cancel his plans," Sara murmured. "I just wanted—"

"He realized that." Cam's gaze was knowing as it followed his brother. "This hasn't been an easy time for Jordan. He's come a long way in a short time and it would be understandable if he did a little backsliding. Don't expect too much from him, Sara, okay?"

"I only want him to come to a party, not achieve

nuclear disarmament," she said dryly. "I don't see what the big deal is."

He took her arm and urged her gently toward his car parked directly behind Jordan's. "You may before the evening is over." His eyes were suddenly twinkling. "And since you've pleaded so prettily for my company, I'll be glad to attend your party."

"Oh, Cam, I'm sorry. I'd be terribly disappointed if you didn't come. It was just that Jordan—"

"Hush. I know." He gave her a sly sidewise glance. "However, if you'd really care to make amends, make sure you invite a few of your most gorgeous women friends to soothe my ego."

"Done." She grinned. "Tall and blond?"

He nodded. "Whatever. I'm easy to please."

She gave an inelegant snort. "Not from what I hear. I'll see if I can find a woman in San Francisco who hasn't heard of your reputation."

"I've only been in town a week. How could I earn a reputation for sexual debauchery in that time?"

"For you that's more than long enough." Her exuberance was returning along with her optimism. Her footsteps quickened. "Come on, there isn't much time. I have people to call and then I should go to the deli and pick up some wonderful cheeses and things." Her brow wrinkled as she tried to remember what she had in her cupboard. "Maybe you could do that for me, Cam. Then I could go to the liquor store and choose the wine."

"First a Don Juan and now an errand boy." He held up his hand to stop her protests. "I'm joking.

I'll be glad to help. I'm sure this will be one hell of a wingding."

"He's not bad," Penny said reluctantly as she gazed across the room at Jordan, who was listening attentively as Rhonda Schwartz described her new sculpture with grandiose gestures. "He's certainly managed to charm everyone in sight tonight."

"And you too," Sara said teasingly. "Admit it, Penny, you like him."

"He's brilliant. His insight on that furor in the Middle East is very impressive." Then as she met Sara's gaze she nodded slowly. "I found him fascinating, witty, and charming. Does that satisfy you?"

Sara shook her head. "I want you to *like* him."

"You don't like a volcano," Penny said dryly. "You admire it for its beauty, respect it for its power, and fear it for its potential. But you don't want to take it home and make a pet of it." Her face softened. "Unless your name is Sara O'Rourke"

"He's changed," Sara said. "He's much more open and free than when I knew him before."

"Are you sure you're not seeing just what you want to see?"

For a moment Sara experienced a flicker of uncertainty. Then, as her gaze returned to Jordan across the room, she was reassured. "No, he's really changed. Jordan used to hate parties. He'd do anything to avoid one. Now look at him. He's actually enjoying himself."

"Is he?" Penny put her glass of wine down on the table beside the door. "Well, he gives that appearance . . . when he's not watching you. I must run along, I have to catch a plane to L.A. early in the morning."

"Watching me?" Sara frowned. "He hasn't been watching me."

"Not obviously, maybe." Penny smiled crookedly. "But I'd bet he knew exactly where you were in this room every moment of the evening. Now, walk me to the elevator like a proper hostess. I want to tell you about the award Kelly O'Brian won for that picture we ran in the last issue."

"That shot of the whale? That was great. Only Kelly could have captured that sense of vulnerability as well as strength." She followed Penny out the door and across the hall to the elevator. "It was mesmerizing."

"Yes, it was." Penny stepped into the elevator. "Good night, Sara. It's been a great party." She turned on the switch and the elevator lurched and then started to move. "But beware of the volcano. I wouldn't want you in the way when he decides to erupt."

Sara laughed. "Penny, he's not going—" She stopped. The elevator had carried Penny out of hearing. Her smile faltered as she felt a frisson of uneasiness. She respected Penny's judgment, but her friend was mistaken this time. Penny didn't understand Jordan or the effort he was making.

She heard a burst of laughter and turned back to the apartment, an eager smile on her lips. No, Penny didn't understand.

Two hours later she closed the door on the last guest and turned to Jordan, sighing contentedly. "It was fun, wasn't it? I love parties." She started to gather up glasses and plates that had been left on the table by the door. "Lord, this place looks like a disaster area. I saw you talking to Raymond Vardeck. Was he trying to sell you one of his paintings? The poor man has been trying to acquire a rich patron for the last two years. He hates the life of a starving artist."

"Then why does he paint?" Jordan picked up two glasses and an hors d'oeuvres tray and followed her to the kitchen.

"Oh, he loves painting, he just hates the starving part. He's pretty good, really. That's one of his paintings over the couch." She stacked the dishes on the cabinet. "I traded him four goulash dinners for it. It's called 'The Chrysanthemum.' "

Jordan dubiously eyed the yellow and orange splotches on the ivory background of the canvas. "I believe one dinner would have been sufficient."

"You're too critical. I like it. It's bright and cheerful." She took the hors d'oeuvres tray from him and set it on the counter. "And it makes me happy to look at it."

A smile lit his face. "Then it's definitely a four-dinner masterpiece." His gaze was searching on her face. "Why did you bother with Vardeck? I know it wasn't for that clumsy painting."

"I felt sorry for him. It's not easy being an art-ist." She started loading the dishwasher. "And he loves my goulash. Anyone who has the good sense to like my cooking at least has the right instincts. When he's not whining, Raymond can be rather sweet."

"And what about the others? You have quite an eclectic group of friends. Artists, sculptors, school-teachers, automobile mechanics."

"I like people," she said simply. "And I find most of them interesting enough to cultivate."

"And they like you." Jordan was regarding her intently. "Whenever I saw you this evening you were surrounded. Someone was always smiling at you, talking to you." He looked away from her. "Touching you."

She carefully positioned a glass in the upper section of the dishwasher. "Penny said she thought you were brilliant."

"I like your friend Penny, but I don't think she likes me."

She poured detergent into the dispenser. "Penny doesn't dislike you. She's just a little wary on my behalf."

Jordan nodded. "She loves you. I don't blame her for not trusting me."

She looked up at him. "You don't?"

"She's intelligent enough to see a good deal that other people don't. What did she say to you?"

Her face lit with amusement. "She called you a volcano."

He chuckled. "I've been called worse. Dormant, I hope?"

"She didn't specify, but I gathered she thought you were reasonably active. I told her she had nothing to worry about."

He went still. "You did?"

"I told her you weren't the same person I knew at Half Moon." She paused. "That I could trust you."

He looked as if she had struck him. "That was . . . generous of you. I thought it would take a great deal longer to convince you I'm treading the virtuous path." He glanced away from her again. "But then, you always were a very trusting person. It made it much easier for me to manipulate you in the past. I would have thought you'd have learned it's dangerous to be so trusting, Sara."

She looked at him in bewilderment. "But you told me to trust you. And you have changed, Jordan. I can see it, *feel* it."

"Not that much." A muscle jumped in his cheek as he turned away. "I've got to get out of here. I'll call you tomorrow."

"What's wrong?" Sara watched him stride across the room. "Jordan, did I say something to—"

"No, you didn't say anything." He opened the door and turned to face her. She inhaled sharply as she saw the torment that tautened his features. "I'm trying. God knows. I'm trying. But I'm only halfway there. Don't trust me too far." His voice suddenly grew harsh. "I like your friends, Sara, but I hated seeing them with you. I didn't want you to smile at them. I don't want you to smile at anyone but me. It rubs me raw to see you—" He stopped and drew a ragged breath. "But you're a woman people will always want to smile at and touch and—" He broke off again. "So I'd better get used to it, hadn't I "

Before she could answer he had closed the door. A moment later she heard the metallic whirr of the elevator. Sara stood quite still, letting his words sink in, weighing the nuances. Then a radiant smile lit her face. He had warned her not to trust him too much and because he had given her that warning it made her trust him all the more.

She began to hum softly as she pressed the button to start the dishwasher.

The message light was lit on Jordan's phone when he returned to the suite. It was a request to return Pedro Marambas's call.

Marambas picked up the receiver on the first ring. "Kemp's flown the coop."

Jordan gripped the receiver so tightly, his knuckles whitened. "When?"

"I'm not sure. Sometime earlier tonight."

"Both you and the New York police were watching him. How could you let him slip away?"

Marambas didn't answer for a moment. "We know we have egg on our faces. I'm not making excuses. The New York police blew it too. Kemp evidently got away clean, but that doesn't mean he's headed for California."

"It doesn't mean that he isn't either," Jordan said grimly. "Have the New York police notified the authorities here?"

"We think so."

"Don't think. Make sure," Jordan said through his teeth. "And I want you to put a watch on the warehouse tonight."

"We've alredy set up additional surveillance. We won't let anything happen to Mrs. Bandor, sir."

"You'd better not. You also assured me you wouldn't let Kemp slip away."

"He shouldn't have been able to get past us. We were working very closely with the local police to avoid any confusion." Marambas's voice betrayed how puzzled he felt. "I don't know how he did it. We're damn good, Mr. Bandor."

"So I understood when I hired you." Jordan's tone was acid with sarcasm. "You'd just better earn that reputation or I'll find a way of blackening it from here to Hong Kong. I don't want my wife so much as frightened by Kemp. Is that clear?"

"I can understand how upset you are but—"

"No, you can't understand. There's no way on earth you can imagine how upset I am, Marambas." Or how frightened, Jordan thought desperately. Bone-chilling terror was icing through him, twisting his guts and making him physically ill. "Keep me informed." He hung up the receiver.

Kemp. He had seen a picture of him in the newspaper and had been filled with a kind of wonder at how ordinary he appeared. Men who killed and mutilated young women should have some hideous marks on their face. Kemp had only looked . . . vacant.

"God," Jordan muttered, "don't let him hurt Sara." It would make no difference to Kemp how loving and giving she was, how she shone with a warmth that was as rare as it was beautiful. He wouldn't care. He would see her only as a victim.

He turned abruptly from the phone and dropped into the easy chair beside the desk. He couldn't let Kemp hurt her. No matter how high the personal price he had to pay, he couldn't let Kemp get to Sara.

Four

"You're getting out of here." Jordan strode past
Sara into the loft. "I wasn't able to get reservations for Sydney until the Qantas flight at ten
tomorrow morning, but we'll move you to my suite
at the Fairmont until then. Where are your suitcases? I'll help you pack." He moved swiftly toward
her bedroom area. "Kemp has slipped away from
the New York police and is probably on his way
here."

"I know," Sara said softly.

He whirled to face her. "How? Did the local
police call you?"

She nodded. "Lieutenant Blaise phoned me a
few hours ago. I guess I don't have to ask how you
found out. All those efficient detectives you have
on your payroll. Well, I suppose it doesn't matter
any longer." She smiled wryly. "Lieutenant Blaise

was very polite and apologized for waking me up. Needless to say, I didn't go back to sleep after I hung up."

"I can see you didn't." His gaze raked her pale face, noting the purple smudges beneath her eyes. He felt a tenderness so intense, it brought a lump to his throat. "Don't worry, I won't let anything happen to you." He turned away. "You don't need to pack everything. I'll have someone send your things on later. Just take enough to last you until—"

"No, Jordan."

He glanced back over his shoulder. "For God's sake, this has nothing to do with anything between us," he said roughly. "I'm not suggesting you move in with me. Well, I am, but not in the sexual sense. I just want to keep you from getting your throat cut. After they've caught Kemp you can come back here and I'll jump through any hoops you set up for me."

"I don't want you to jump through any hoops." Her voice was low. "And I told you last night that I trusted you."

"Then you'll come with me?"

"I can't," she said wearily. "Heaven knows I want to come, but it's not possible. Not right now."

He gazed at her in disbelief. "It has to be now. You've got to get out of her. This place is an open invitation to Kemp."

"That's why I moved in here."

He froze. "I beg your pardon." Each word was

enunciated with great precision. "I don't believe I heard you correctly."

"The police were getting nowhere trying to dig up new evidence to convict Kemp, but they knew they had one last avenue to explore." She gestured to herself. "Kemp's psychological profile indicates that he probably would attempt to carry out his threat against me. So the New York police and the local authorities here decided to join forces and try to get him on an attempt charge if there was no other solution."

"Bait," he breathed softly. "My God, you're letting them use you for bait."

'It's the only way we can think of to get him off the streets. It's only a matter of time before he kills again. He's like a time bomb set to go off." She shivered. "While I was doing that story I studied him. I know what Kemp is."

"And you've set yourself up to go off with him when he explodes."

"It won't be like that." Sara frowned. "Lieutenant Blaise is very competent. He assured me—"

"Don't tell me about competence," Jordan interrupted harshly. "Not when they've just let Kemp slip through their fingers . . ." He stopped as the realization dawned on him. "They *let* him go. Those idiots turned their backs and let him go."

Sara nodded. "They considered it the best psychological moment. Kemp's frustration has been steadily building and—"

"All very logical and cerebral," Jordan bit out.

"Your Lieutenant Blaise has it worked out, hasn't he? If Kemp does come and they manage to capture him before he murders you, he gets him on an attempt charge. And if he does murder you, he gets him on an even bigger rap. Either way the long arm of the law wins and everybody gets promotions. And I suppose *World Report* will be overjoyed to get the exclusive no matter who's alive to write it."

"It's not like that. No one is forcing me to do this. I agreed of my own free will." She made a face. "And Penny and Mac would have a fit if they knew I was involved in this situation."

"Then tell the police you've changed your mind. Tell them you're not going to play their little cat-and-mouse game." He took a step nearer. "*Tell* them."

She shook her head. "He's killed four women, Jordan. Perhaps even more that we don't know about yet. I can't let him take another life."

"It's not your responsibility. It's the police who—" He stopped. Her expression held absolute determination. "Okay, let them use you, but not like this. Move to my suite at the Fairmont. Don't make it so easy for Kemp. Let me be there to protect you."

"And endanger you? I couldn't live with myself if I did that, Jordan."

"You may not live at all if you—" He broke off, trying to get hold of himself, trying to subdue the terror rising within him. "Stop being so damn brave. Let me *help* you."

"I'm not brave," she whispered. "I'm scared to death. I watched his face in that courtroom for four solid weeks. He's not sane, Jordan."

He moved instantly to take advantage of any hint of weakness. "Then he probably won't do what those nice logical policemen think he will. How can they protect you if they don't know which way he'll jump?"

She moistened her dry lips with her tongue. "Please, I'm frightened enough as it is. And I *will* do this, Jordan.'

"Sara, dammit, you can't . . ." He trailed off. It was no use. No matter what he said, he could see he wasn't going to be able to change her mind. "Tell me what I can do. Tell me how I can keep you alive."

"You can't do anything. Stay out of it and let the police handle it." She met his gaze. "I don't want you to come near me for the next few days."

He stared at her, feeling the pain and panic swelling within him like a tidal wave. "I don't know if I can do that. This is all crazy, Sara."

"Sometimes that's the way life is. Crazy and scary and . . ." She drew a shaky breath and forced herself to smile. "I think you'd better leave now. Lieutenant Blaise is going to be here in another fifteen minutes to discuss the surveillance."

"I'll stay and talk to the bastard."

"No," she said sharply. "You're out of this. This is my business and I'm the one who's going to take care of it."

"The hell I will. I'll—" He stopped as he saw the

wariness in her face. She hadn't looked at him like this since that first night. He was pushing her, destroying the fledgling trust he'd nurtured so carefully. Why had this crisis had to come so soon? One false step and he could blow everything he had built between them. It was a catch-22 that made his frustration and fear escalate to new heights. His voice was hoarse. "Look, Sara, I can't take this. I can't *stand* the thought of your being hurt."

"You have to stand it," she said quietly. "Just as I do. If you want to help me, you'll go now."

He stood looking at her for a long moment and then turned and headed for the front door. "I do want to help you. I've *got* to help you." He opened the door and glanced back over his shoulder. "Nothing in the whole damn world is more important to me than keeping you alive. Nothing, Sara."

The door shut behind him with a forcefulness that held a hint of violence.

Sara sank down on the couch, her arms folded across her chest, hugging herself. She felt suddenly cold, isolated, now that Jordan had left. Lord, she hadn't wanted to send him away. The temptation to go into his arms and let him hold her, protect her, had been nearly overpowering. She knew how strong Jordan was both physically and mentally, and it would have been wonderful to be able to lean on him when she was so frightened.

But she couldn't lean on him if it meant putting him in danger. The very idea terrified her even more than facing Kemp alone. No, there was no way she could have let Jordan stay and give her the comfort she wanted so desperately.

A knock sounded on the door. Lieutenant Blaise, she thought numbly. She would have to ask him to identify himself before she opened the door. He had a key to the lift, but told her not to open the door unless she was certain she knew who was on the other side. She got up from the couch and moved swiftly across the room toward the front door.

"Marambas called again," Cam said as soon as Jordan walked into the suite. "He said to tell you he'd contacted his informant in the office of the New York police and there was something weird going on with the surveillance crew that was shadowing Kemp. It seems they intentionally distracted our people and—"

"Let him go," Jordan finished for him as he threw himself into a chair. "What else did he say?"

"You knew?"

"It was a setup." Jordan's lips tightened. "With Sara as the sacrificial lamb. A very willing lamb."

"No wonder you look so uptight."

"That's a massive understatement. If they pretended to lose Kemp, they must have arranged to keep a tail on him. Has Kemp reached San Francisco yet?"

Cam shook his head. "And he won't be here for at least another forty-eight hours. Evidently, he's low on funds and bought a bus ticket from New York to San Francisco. It's due in at the Greyhound station at 3:05 P.M. day after tomorrow. Marambas said to tell you his operative flew to St. Louis and will board Kemp's bus there."

Forty-eight hours. Kemp was coming, Jordan thought. There had been the slightest hope that Kemp might have decided not to make good on his threat, but now that hope was gone.

"What are you going to do?" Cam asked quietly. "Can't you persuade Sara to get the hell out of this town?"

"No." Jordan's hands clenched on the arms of the chair. "She says she can't let Kemp stay out on the street. She won't even let me stay with her or help her." He covered his eyes with his hand. It was trembling. "God, I'm scared."

"The police will protect her," Cam said. "I guess you'll have to trust them."

Jordan's hand dropped again to the arm of the chair. "That's easy to say. Would you be willing to sit on the sidelines if it was your wife they were using as bait?"

Cam hesitated. "No, I guess we're both too possessive to rely on anyone else to protect what belongs to us. It must be a Bandor family trait." He paused. "But what else can you do?"

"Well, I'm sure as hell not going to rest on my duff and do nothing." Jordan stood up and headed for the front door. "I'm going back to Sara's apartment and I'm staying there until they catch Kemp."

"You said she wouldn't let you stay with her."

"I'll find a way."

A flicker of apprehension crossed Cam's face. "Be careful, Jordan. For God's sake, don't lose the ground you've already gained. It may be too soon to—"

"Do you think I don't know that?" Jordan's expression was bleak. "I have to take my chances. It's better that I lose Sara than for Sara to lose her life."

"Jordan . . ." Cam trailed off. What else could he say? He would probably do the same thing in Jordan's place. "If I can help, let me know."

"Just stay here in case Marambas calls again. Contact me right away if there's any news about Kemp."

"I won't budge until you come back." Cam hesitated. "You'll be at Sara's all night?"

"Yes," Jordan lips tightened. "I'll be at Sara's."

"Here take one of these sacks. I don't want to crush your treasures." He thrust a grocery bag into Sara's hand and strode past her into the apartment. "Lord, it's raining hard. I was lucky the sacks didn't burst open in the supermarket parking lot. They're soggy as hell."

Sara quickly smothered the sudden leap of joy she had felt when Jordan had identified himself and she had opened the door to see him standing there. "What are you doing here? I told you—"

"To stay away from you." Jordan gave her a flashing smile over his shoulder. "And I will, when the trap is ready to be sprung. But I'm sure your Lieutenant Blaise has told you that you don't have to worry about Kemp for another forty-eight hours. Why should I have to eat dinner alone when there's no reason that you can't join me?" He set two bags down on the kitchen counter. "Or rather I can join you. We'd both be drowned if we tried to make it to a restaurant."

He pulled off his olive crewneck sweater and tossed it on one of the kitchen stools. The white shirt he wore beneath it was almost as wet as the sweater and clung like a second skin to his lean body. She could see the shadow of the dark hair feathering his chest through the damp shirt and had a sudden heated memory of the springy texture of that thatch as it touched her bare breasts.

She forced her gaze away from his chest and up to his face. "I don't think this is a very good idea."

"You have to eat." He began unpacking the groceries. "Of course, you could send one of the policemen in the unmarked car across the street to the nearest Burger King." He looked up and smiled. His dark hair was rumpled and slightly damp and the eye not covered by the black patch was twinkling. He looked like a mischievous pirate, and a melting tenderness touched her. "Now, wouldn't you rather have one of these?" He rummaged in the sack until he found two cellophane-wrapped steaks and held them up triumphantly. "Did I ever tell you what a fantastic bush cook I am? I can do things with herbs and seasonings that will blow your mind."

"You know how to cook?" Intrigued, she closed the door and moved toward him. "No, you know very well you never told me. You know everything about me and I know practically nothing about you." She sat down on one of the stools at the breakfast bar, gazing at him eagerly. "Did you spend much time in the outback?"

He lowered his gaze to the steak in his hands. "Pretty much. We didn't always live at Half Moon Bay." He ripped off the cellophane and turned on the broiler. "Until I was thirteen we had a station two hundred miles north of Adelaide. We barely eked out a living on the property, and my father and I earned extra money taking tourists into the outback to see 'the glories of the land down under.'" He made a face. "God, I hated it. All I wanted to do was stay at home on Bandora and build our station into the best damn property in Australia."

Jordan had never confided anything about his childhood and she was almost afraid to speak, afraid he would stop and withdraw from her again. "Bandora was the name of your station?"

Jordan nodded as he continued to unload the groceries. "My father said that someday our name would be sung from one end of the country to the other when we made Bandora all that it could be. How he loved that station."

"And so did you," she murmured, gazing at his face.

A sudden bitterness touched his lips. "Oh, yes, I loved it. Maybe even more than my father. We ate, slept, and breathed Bandora." He crushed the empty paper bag and threw it in the wastebasket beside the cabinet. "Neither of us could think of anything else."

She felt a tiny thrill of excitement. She was coming so close. He had revealed more of his past to her in the last few moments than he had during the entire period of their marriage. If she was patient, surely he would give her the key to understanding him. "Did Cam live at Bandora too?"

"Not during the rough years. Those times were over when my father married his mother." He looked up. "Where can I find a grill to put these steaks on?"

"In the cabinet." She gestured to the doors below the sink. "Cam is your stepbrother? Why didn't you ever tell me?"

"It wasn't important. Cam is as close as any real brother to me and my father legally adopted him."

It was important. Everything he was telling her was an important revelation that was ripping aside the barriers and the mystery that had kept her from knowing Jordan. "When did you move to Half Moon Bay?"

"Why don't we talk about it later?" He gave her a surprisingly boyish smile over his shoulder as he knelt to find the grill. "To maintain my reputation I've got to concentrate on making you the best steak you've ever eaten." He peered into the cabinet. "I don't see a grill. Are you sure it's here? Oh, there it is." He drew out the grill and stood up with one lithe movement.

His damp jeans were clinging to the strong line of his thighs, she suddenly noticed worriedly. He'd probably catch cold standing there in those wet clothes. "Why are you worrying about those blasted steaks, when you'll be lucky if you don't get pneumonia?" She plopped the bag he had given her when he'd entered the apartment onto the breakfast bar and slipped from the stool. "I'll put the steaks on while you go into the bathroom and towel off and use my hair dryer. Then light a fire in the fireplace and bake some of the dampness out of those clothes."

"I'm not that wet. I'll wait until—"

"Go," she said firmly as she went behind the counter and took the grill from him. "Now."

A tiny smile tugged at his lips. "Yes, ma'am." He turned toward the bathroom. "But you don't know the culinary experience you're missing by riding roughshod over my humble person." He glanced back over his shoulder and solemnly winked his right eye. "You do know that it was all a plot?"

Her eyes widened warily. "A plot?"

He nodded solemnly. "I hired a pilot to seed the clouds and cause a cloudburst to place you in just this dilemma. I can't really cook a great beefsteak." He opened the door to the bathroom. "I'm much better with kangaroo meat."

The smile was still lingering on Sara's lips as the door closed behind him. She shook her head as she turned and placed the grill under the broiler. She had never known Jordan to behave with such boyish lightheartedness. She was glad she had decided to let him stay for dinner. But had she decided or had she been swept along on the wave of Jordan's personality? She frowned with sudden apprehension. She didn't like the idea of being swept anywhere against her wishes, and the phrase brought back too many memories of Jordan's manipulation of her in the past.

Still, the decision hadn't really been against her will. She desperately wanted to find out more of Jordan's past and he wasn't treating her as he had before. His demeanor had been companionable, even sweet. Not calculated and sensual. No, she was being too wary of Jordan's motives. He had come because he wanted to give comfort. He hadn't wanted her to be alone with her fear and dread.

She began to season the steaks, her heart lighter and more full of hope than at any time since she had heard that Kemp had left New York.

"Tell me more about Bandora." Sara snuggled deeper into the softness of the cushioned couch and gazed dreamily into the depths of the fire. "You said it wasn't like Half Moon?"

Jordan shook his head before lifting his glass to his lips. "Night and day. Nothing was easy there. The land was hard and unforgiving." He gazed down into the ruby depths of his wine. "So were the people who lived there." He abruptly set his glass on the end table beside him, stood up, and crossed to the fireplace. "There's nothing much to tell." He picked up the poker and briskly stoked the logs until the sparks flew. "Not much happens in the outback."

But Sara had an idea something very important had happened to Jordan at Bandora. The sudden tension that wired his every movement was sending out clear signals that she was effortlessly picking up. She was beginning to be able to read him, she realized contentedly. He was no longer the enigma that had both fascinated and intimidated her. In the last week he had shown a vulnerable side that had touched her as his more forceful persona never had. "How old did you say you were when your mother died?"

He stopped in mid-action as he stirred the logs. "Twelve." Then he straightened and replaced the poker before turning and smiling at her. "How about another glass of wine?"

The subject was evidently closed, Sara realized with disappointment. Well, she had learned a great deal this evening and must not be impatient. "I don't think so. Two is my limit." She placed her empty glass on the end table. "Thank you, Jordan.'

"For what? You're the one who cooked dinner."

She shook her head. "For being here when I needed you. For helping me through a bad time."

"You would have made it without me." He crossed back to her and dropped to his knees beside the couch. He deliberately exaggerated his Australian drawl, "You're one strong sheila, mate."

"You said that before but sometimes I don't feel very strong." And this was one of the times, Sara thought. She was excruciatingly sensitive to her own physical vulnerability, her skin that could be bruised and marked, her vitality that could be quenched in the flicker of an eye.

"Listen." Jordan's voice was soft but his gaze held her own with mesmerizing intensity. "Do you know what I thought when I first saw you? Summer. You reminded me of summer on Bandora. Gentle mornings, hot afternoons and the nights—" His index finger touched her cheek. "Unbelievable."

Her skin couldn't be throbbing beneath that light touch, she thought hazily, it must be her imagination. Then his finger moved slowly down her cheek to the corner of her lips and she gasped. Her lips felt suddenly swollen, and the nipples of her breasts blossomed, hardened, against the soft knit of her T-shirt.

"Summer has many moods, but underneath every one of them is always the warmth and the strength. When I got to know you, I found you were exactly what I had thought you were." His finger traveled down her neck to the hollow of her throat. The pulse leapt beneath the pad of his finger. Her lungs were constricting and her breasts were lifting and falling as she tried to get her breath. "Sunlight. You warmed me." His head bent slowly until his lips hovered over her own. "Heat. You burned me."

He was the one who was burning her, Sara thought. The heat emanating from her body was seeping into her blood, into every muscle, into her bones. She was melting. "Jordan . . ."

"Shh . . ." His palm covered her right breast. "I want to feel your heart beat for me." He bent and laid his dark head on her left breast. "I want to *hear* it." His hand gently, rhythmically, squeezed her right breast, his thumb teasingly flicking the hard nipple. Her heart was beating so hard, she felt as if it were about to leap from her chest.

"I love this,"Jordan whispered. "Being close to you, touching you. You're all sunlight and life." His lips moved a fraction of an inch, and he pressed his warm tongue to her nipple. She shuddered. The thin cotton knit might as well have not been there for all the difference it made. "Sara, I'm hurting so."

So was she. The emptiness between her thighs was aching, throbbing to be filled. She couldn't *stand* it. She pushed him away and tore the T-shirt over her head, baring her breasts. He watched her, his gaze intent, his lips heavy with sensuality.

Then his mouth was on her bare breast, sucking strongly, his hands cupping, framing, as his teeth and tongue took and took and took. She moaned deep in her throat, her spine arching helplessly, her fingers clutching at his thick hair. "Jordan, I've got to—" She broke off as his teeth tugged gently at her nipple, exerting just enough pressure to bring sharp pleasure with no pain. "Jordan, now!"

"Not yet." His deft fingers moved swiftly on the zipper of her jeans as his lips went to her other breast. "I want it to be so good for you, love. You know you have to be ready before you're able to take me." He slipped her jeans and panties down and off her. "I don't want to hurt you." His fingers were between her thighs now, swiftly finding what he sought. "I can't stand the thought of you being hurt, Sara."

She was hurting now, she thought desperately. His thumb was pressing, rotating. Her neck arched back against the pillows of the couch as her lips parted to force more air into her starved lungs.

"Just a little more, love," he murmured. His fingers suddenly plunged. "That's right, flow. Cling to me." Another finger slipped into her silken warmth. She was full, yet she needed . . . Jordan knew what she needed. Jordan always knew.

"Enough." Jordan's nostrils were flaring, and there was a flush mantling his cheeks. His chest was moving heavily with the harshness of his breathing. "Dear heaven, I hope it's enough, I can't wait any longer." With trembling fingers he unbuttoned his shirt, his gaze never leaving her face. "Tell me you need me, Sara. I have to hear you say it."

He had to know already, Sara thought hazily. She was lying here naked before him, her body exquisitely tuned to the siren's song of desire he had woven upon it, her breasts heavy and ripe, waiting for his mouth, his tongue.

"Tell me," he urged softly, stripping off his shirt and throwing it aside. The black hair of the triangle on his chest looked soft, springy, and she suddenly leaned forward and undulated her upper body against him. "I want you," she whispered. "I want this."

The dark thatch was as erotically abrasive as she remembered against her sensitive nipples, and her nails dug spasmodically into his shoulders. "I've missed you so, Jordan."

His arms went around her, his palms going down to cup her buttocks.

"Oh, God, Sara, I've been so empty inside." His voice was muffled in her hair. "My body has never stopped hurting for you, but that's only part of it." His hoarse laugh had an edge of desperation. "Though it's a damn big part at the moment and getting bigger every minute." He pushed her away and quickly unzipped his jeans. "As you'll soon learn, love."

"Let me help you."

"No," he said sharply, rising to his feet. "Don't touch me. It's been too long." He was quickly stripping. "Stay there. Just let me look at you." His lips twisted ruefully. "Though that's a form of torture in itself at the moment."

She knew exactly what he meant. Jordan was naked now, the firelight burnishing his slim, muscular body with a copper glow. He was so beautifully male, beautifully sensual. She felt the muscles of her belly clench as her gaze followed the arrow of dark hair down his chest, past his flat belly.

"It will be all right," he said quietly as he followed her gaze. "You're ready for me now." He dropped to the floor before her, parting her legs and slipping between them. His fingers probed, teased, and proved his words beyond any shadow of doubt. "Sara . . ." His cheek was rubbing against her breast, the faint bristle of a shadowy growth brushing her softness, arousing her in yet another way. "Let me have you. I *have* to have you."

She gasped as he pulled her down on the floor, cushioning her against the fall with his own body. Flesh against flesh. Shock tingled through her and then a bigger shock electrified her as he plunged into her with one powerful thrust.

So full. Deliciously full. She couldn't move. But she didn't need to move. Jordan was moving both of them, lifting, stroking, thrusting with a wild primeval energy.

Her teeth were gritting to keep from screaming as sensation after sensation tore through her. She tried but she couldn't keep a low keening moan from escaping.

Jordan smiled up at her, his lips wonderfully tender even in their fierce sensuality. "Do you know how often in the past months I've woken from a sound sleep because I thought I heard you make that little half moan?" he asked thickly. He rolled them over, taking his weight on his strong arms when she was under him. Then he plunged deeply, watching her face to catch every nuance of expression. "And then not be able to go back to sleep because I wanted you so much that it was an ache that twisted my guts."

She gasped as he thrust harder.

He frowned in concern. "Too much?"

"No." She began to meet his movements with ones of her own. "More!"

He covered her lips with his own, his tongue plunging, his hips plunging. Heat was building. She heard a low groan but she didn't know if it came from him or her. It didn't matter. They were one. Plunging, burning, reaching.

She could hear the sound of his harsh breathing above her, the power of his thrusts escalated until she was weak. Molten. His.

His face above her was taut as he fought for control, waiting for her. But he didn't have to wait long, the tension was too great, the pace too hot. The release of that tension exploded violently in a white-hot burst of rapture.

"Sara." Jordan breathed with relief. "I was afraid . . ." Then he kissed her softly, sweetly. "I wasn't sure I could hold on. I've been wanting you for too long."

That was strange. She couldn't ever remember Jordan voicing doubts, particularly in the area of lovemaking, where he was so unequivocally a master. But this was a new Jordan, vulnerable and more open and . . . sweet, she thought drowsily. "Wonderful."

"Yes, it was." He kissed her and rolled with her onto their sides. "And it's going to be even more wonderful for us the next time, now that the edge is off." He stood up and reached down to draw her to her feet. "Come on, first we're going to shower and then I'm going to watch you open the presents you've so rudely ignored." He nodded at the grocery sack she'd set on the breakfast bar before dinner and completely forgotten. "I think you should be taught a few manners, Madame Bandor."

"Presents? I don't want any gifts. I told you—"

"Hush." Jordan's arm slipped around her waist as he propelled her toward the bathroom. "These are very special and you'll have no qualms about accepting these particular gifts. I promise you, love."

"But I . . ." She trailed off and gave up the battle. She was too happy to quarrel with him at the moment. She would worry about his penchant for giving extravagant gifts after their shower. "We'll have to take turns. My shower stall is the size of a postage stamp."

"I noticed that while I was drying my hair," he said, his bright blue eye twinkled mischievously. "And we definitely will *not* take turns." His hand slid up from her waist to cup one breast in his palm. "I do enjoy a nice cozy shower."

She felt suddenly breathless. "We'll be right on top of each other."

"I do hope so, love." He opened the glass shower door. "That's exactly the position I have in mind."

Five

Jordan dried himself sketchily, took the shower cap off Sara, and fluffed up her hair. Then he turned away, tossing her a bath towel. "Dry off, I'll be right back."

"Where are you going?"

"To get your robe. I want to be sure you're suitably dressed for the occasion."

Sara found herself smiling as she began to run the terry towel over her stomach. That was a switch, Sara thought, Jordan had appeared to be delighted to undress her for this particular occasion. *Delight.* What a delicious word and one that described her mood exactly. Delight that soared and sparkled, laughter that bubbled and flowed.

"I was hoping you'd still have this robe. It was stashed in the back of your closet." Jordan was back and carrying her thigh-length happi coat over one arm. "I remember how pretty you looked in it."

"I'd forgotten I had it." Jordan had purchased the exquisite silk garment in Singapore on a business trip a few months after their marriage. The brilliant yellow of the material shimmered under the light in a blaze of exotic beauty. The silk was cool against her flesh as she slipped it on. "I haven't worn it in months."

"Eighteen?" His voice was low as he carefully smoothed the front of the robe. Then he smiled with an effort and said, "Don't answer that. I don't want to think about those months tonight." He whirled and pulled her out of the bathroom. "Come on, it's present time."

She was half-laughing, half-protesting as he propelled her across the room to the dhurrie rug in front of the fireplace. He gathered two of the beige cushions from the couch and tossed them on the floor. "Sit." He strode toward the breakfast bar to get the sack.

She fell on her knees on the cushions and sat back on her heels. "Jordan, you're so damn stubborn. Why won't you listen to me? I don't want—"

"You have to accept these or you'll hurt my feelings." He was coming back carrying the paper sack. He fell to his knees and pulled out a gaudy gold foil party hat with a yellow plume. He settled the golden cornet on her head. "I crown you Queen Sara," he said solemnly. "Queen of the May."

Sara found herself giggling. "Well, it's certainly different from the last gift you gave me. I feel like one of those flappers from the twenties."

He shook his head. "A queen," he repeated gravely. He reached into the sack again. "And here's your scepter."

She burst out laughing. It was a yellow plastic back scratcher with four curved prongs on one end and a huge metallic bow taped to the long handle. "Jordan, you idiot."

He pretended to be hurt. "You don't like it? I thought it quite royal-looking."

"Oh, very royal." Her eyes were dancing as she took the scepter and waved it with a grand gesture. "If you were dressed more appropriately for the ceremony, I'd knight you."

"Oh, but I couldn't accept it." He smiled innocently. "Not yet. A knight has to earn his spurs. But if you'll wear my favors in the tournament, I'm sure I'd be able to win them."

"Tournament?"

He nodded solemnly. "Of course. Every queen has to have a tournament." His smile deepened into sensuality. "We're about to have one helluva bloody tournament." He paused. "If her majesty permits."

The firelight cast shadows over the planes of his face and glinted on his dark hair. The playfulness had vanished, replaced by a sensuality so intense, she could feel it vibrating, encompassing, and holding her helpless in its field. She swallowed. "I don't know much about tournaments."

"We'll learn together. Will you wear my favors?"

"I thought it was the knight who wore the favors."

"Not necessarily." He was reaching into the sack again. "Who says we can't make our own rules."

"You always do." Her voice sounded breathless and she found herself shivering with anticipation. She wanted to touch him. She wanted his hands on her body. The urgency of the desire was no surprise. Jordan had always been able to arouse her to instant sexual response. Many things had altered in their relationship, but that had remained steadfast. "Why should this be any different?" Her gaze dropped to a cellophane twisted into a cone shape. "Flowers?"

"Very special flowers." He tore off the cellophane. "Daisies. I thought they were pretty and very appropriate for the Queen of the May."

The yellow daisies were bright and cheerful and rather sweet. She took a flower from the bunch. "I'll be glad to wear your favor." She started to weave it into her hair, but he reached out and stopped her.

"No," he said softly as he took the daisy from her. "Not there. It would distract from your crown."

She felt heat tingle through her and it was suddenly painful to draw a breath. "Where, then?"

He held her gaze as he smiled slowly.

Her heart began to pound harder. "Jordon . . ."

With a deliberate movement he parted the edges of the happi coat and pushed it away from her body. "We'll have to find a place for every one of these daisies." He tilted his head to study the lush curves of her naked body. "Now, where do you plant daisies? On a hill perhaps . . ."

He had her lie down, then placed a daisy over her left breast just above the nipple. "How does it feel? It looks so beautiful. We have to plant a field. . . . He scattered daisy heads all over her body. "Pretty. So pretty."

Her breasts and belly with their daisy decorations trembled with her every breath. Hot color was stinging her cheeks and burning through every vein.

"Such a lovely garden. Such a lovely Sara," Jordan murmured.

The emptiness between her thighs was throbbing, aching to be filled. "When does the tournament start?"

"Soon." He bent his head slowly, his breath feathering one pointed, distended nipple. "Just a few preliminary forays . . ." His lips closed on her nipple and he sucked delicately. A low cry broke from her and she reached out for him. He lifted his head and smiled as he took her hands and put them back at her sides. "No, just lie there and let me tease you a little. It will make it better for you."

"Tease me a *little*!" She was burning up, lost in a haze of hunger. It was sheer sensual torture to lie here unmoving while Jordan's lips and teeth tugged and soothed, tugged again . . .

It couldn't last much longer; Jordan's chest was heaving as if he were running and his cheeks were hollowed with hunger. He was whispering her name over and over in a husky litany.

He suddenly plunged forward, filling her.

Sara's lips opened in a silent scream and her nails

dug into the muscles of his shoulders. He laughed softly. "Every Queen of the May is entitled to a maypole. I hope you like yours, Sara."

Fever. Beauty. Golden daisies in a field of rapture. "Yes, oh, yes."

"Then let the tournament begin."

It was wilder than the time before, wilder than anything she had ever imagined. Heat, force, tension. Then the tournament ended with a passionate explosion that made them both the victors.

Sara collapsed against him. She couldn't move, every muscle felt like warm butter. She could hear the thunder of Jordan's heart slowing beneath her ear but he, too, was trembling. His palm was stroking, caressing her back in a movement that was poignantly sweet after the storm that had gone before. "Sara?"

She didn't have breath enough to answer.

"Come on, love. Bed." He lifted her off him and rose to his feet before pulling her up to stand beside him. Daisy petals drifted from her body as she swayed unsteadily.

"Oops." He scooped her up in his arms and carried her toward the bedroom area. "Tournaments can be exhausting, can't they, love?"

"I can walk," she protested, but weakly.

"I want you to save your strength." He grinned down at her. "You're obviously out of training for this kind of tournament, and I want you fresh for the next event."

"Is that a slam at my sexual stamina?"

His smile deepened to tenderness. "Oh, no, I'm

happy as a clam you've been leading the celibate life. I'd have shown up here a helluva lot sooner if I'd thought there was any danger of you jousting with any other man. Fortunately, you shied away from relationships after you left me. Not exactly a compliment but . . ." His expression became grave. "There hasn't been any other woman since you left me. I want you to know that, Sara."

She gazed at him, stunned. She knew how highly sexed Jordan was and yet it was clear he was telling her the truth. "I . . . see." She didn't know what to say, and she felt suddenly shy, awkward, and tried to lighten the moment. "Well, then it's no wonder you fell down on the efficiency level."

He laid her down on the bed. "I wasn't aware that I did."

"The daisies. You didn't scatter them all, as you said you would."

He lay down beside her and propped his head on his hand, gazing down at her. His lips curved in a teasing smile. "I'm saving the last two for later. I know exactly where I'm going to plant those particular daisies."

"You do?"

His head lowered slowly until their lips were just a breath away. "Oh, yes, love, I most certainly do!"

Sara stirred, fighting her way through the skeins of sleep. There was something wrong. No, not wrong. Just not . . . right. She opened her eyes, her gaze searching the darkness. "Jordan?"

"I'm here." He quickly moved closer, leaning on one elbow to look down at her. "I'll always be here."

His features were shadowy above her, but she could sense the tension emanating from him. "Can't you sleep?"

"I didn't try." His fingers stroked the fair hair back from her temple with exquisite tenderness. "I wanted to savor this. It's been so long since I've lain beside you. I wanted to store up the memories."

Sadness. The aching sadness in his tone engendered a concern that brought Sara fully awake. "There *is* something wrong. What—"

His lips were covering her own with gentle sweetness. He lifted his head. "How could anything be wrong as long as we have this? Nothing could be more right than the two of us together." He kissed her again and when he spoke again his voice was soft, urgent. "You can see that, can't you? You have to let me stay with you."

The hint of desperation in his voice caused her uneasiness to return. "What are you saying? I don't know what—"

He was kissing her again and it was no longer gentle, no longer sweet but hot, hard, sensual. "Shh, never mind," he said. His tongue entered, stroked, teased as his hands began their magic arousal of her body. "Don't worry about it. Don't worry about anything but this."

"But, Jordon, tell me . . ." She trailed off, forgetting words, forgetting thought, remembering only sensation.

The phone rang, once more rousing Sara from sleep.

"I'll get it," Jordan said quickly as he started to reach across her. "Go back to sleep."

"Don't be silly," she said, pushing his arm away. "The phone is on my side of the bed." She reached out and picked up the receiver. "Hello."

"Sara?" It was Cam's voice. "Sorry to wake you, but I have to speak to Jordan. Will you put him on?"

"Cam?" She sat up in bed and shook her head to clear it of sleep. "How did you know—"

"It's Cam?" Jordan took the phone away from her and spoke into the receiver. "What the devil is wrong now, Cam?"

Wrong? Sara slowly lifted the telephone cord and slipped under it and out of bed. Oh, yes, something was wrong all right and not only the information Cam was imparting to Jordan. Something was terribly, terribly wrong. She slipped on the yellow happi coat and shivered a little as the cool silk touched her body. Strange, she hadn't thought she could feel any colder. The needle of ice that had pierced through her when the pieces had all come together seemed to be spreading into every cell of her body.

"You're sure?" Jordan's voice was clipped. "There's no mistake?"

Oh, God, how could *she* have made such a mistake? Sara wondered. How could she have been so stupid, so blasted trusting? She turned on the lamp beside the phone on the bedside table. The sudden illumination caused Jordan to blink, and his gaze flew to Sara standing by the bed. His expression became wary. "Tell Marambas. I want him found," he said, his gaze never leaving Sara's face. "Even if he has to backtrack to every stop. I'll talk to you later, Cam." He replaced the receiver on the cradle and sat very still, looking at her with narrowed eyes. "Well?"

"I want you to leave." Her voice was trembling. "I want you to get dressed and leave and not come back. Not ever."

A flicker of pain crossed his face and then was gone. "Aren't you overreacting?"

"Overreacting?" The icy cold was gone, burned away by fury. "Do you think I'm an idiot? Cam *knew* you were here. I could tell. There wasn't the slightest doubt in his mind that you'd be in bed beside me and I'd be able to hand the phone to you. Now, how could he know, Jordan?" Her hands clenched into fists at her sides. "Unless you told him you planned on being here all night? And you did tell him that, didn't you? You had every intention of making sure you seduced me when you walked through my front door tonight."

His face was pale in the lamplight. "Yes, I did. Every intention. I won't lie to you, Sara."

She crossed her arms across her breasts to try to still the trembling. "You manipulated me to get your own way. You knew I wasn't ready for this but you decided—" She laughed shakily. "Damn, but you're good. You played me so well that I didn't have a chance. You were so blasted honest and boyish. You even dangled those little tidbits about Bandora in front of me and I snapped at the bait like a hungry trout. You were sure I would, weren't you? You know I've always been curious about you."

"Yes, I knew you wanted to know more about me." He got out of bed and strode out of the bedroom area. A moment later he returned with the clothes he'd left strewn on the carpet before the fireplace and began to dress. "And yes, I used every bit of knowledge I had as to what makes you tick to get you to let me stay with you tonight." He looked up as he began to button his white shirt. "And I would have continued to try seduction or guile or any other weapon I possessed to make you let me stay with you until Kemp was caught. I told you I couldn't stand the thought of your being hurt."

"And I told you I'd never be manipulated by you again. I was wrong." She laughed huskily. "Oh, boy, was I wrong. You would have thought I'd have learned my lesson. You're such a skilled teacher, Jordan. Well, no more. I think I've at last seen the light at the end of the tunnel. You were right; I was far too trusting."

"I suppose it wouldn't be any use to remind you these circumstances are unusual and might never occur again?" He looked searchingly at her. "No, I can see it wouldn't." His smile was bittersweet. "I didn't think I'd get lucky." He fastened his belt and thrust his feet into his loafers. "I knew when I came here tonight it was probably going to blow everything."

Her lips tightened. "How perceptive of you. If you used those methods now, knowing that they could destroy our relationship, you'd use them anytime to get what you want."

"Would I?" He shook his head. "I don't think I would have, Sara. I think I was actually on the road to giving you what you wanted from me." He shrugged. "Not that you'll believe that either now."

For a moment she was shaken out of her rage and bitterness by the aura of pain surrounding him that reached out and enfolded her. Then her own pain rushed back and she deliberately closed her mind to what he was feeling. She would *not* feel sorry for him. He had used her, molded her as if she were Galatea to his Pygmalion. "Why should I? You can't expect me to believe anything you say."

"No, I can't expect anything of you. I'm not fool enough to think I'll get another chance from you. You warned me, didn't you?"

"Yes."

"So I have nothing more to lose." He smiled with sudden recklessness. "I'm free to do any damn thing I choose. No more walking on eggs, no more worrying about what you'll think of me."

"I don't care what you do." Oh, dear heaven, she wished that were true. This was a thousand times more agonizing than the first parting. She felt as if she were bleeding inside, but the icy rage was cauterizing and making it bearable.

Jordan turned a shade paler, but his smile never wavered. "Good. That makes everything much simpler for me." He turned on his heel. "Good-bye, Sara. Come lock the door behind me."

She followed him from the bedroom and watched as he crossed the loft. The flames in the fireplace had burned down to glowing embers and cast an eerie red glow on Jordan's face, giving his features a strange, satanic beauty. He unlocked and opened the door before turning to face her. "In case you're interested, Kemp got off the Greyhound bus somewhere between New York and St. Louis. He could have caught a plane or a train or another bus. At any rate, your efficient policemen aren't going to be able to pick up his trail very easily." His gaze met Sara's across the room. "He could be here in two hours or two days. I'll tell the detectives on stakeout downstairs to be on guard, but don't unlock your door tonight without checking. Not for anyone."

"I won't," she whispered. "Just leave, Jordan."

"I'm leaving." He stood looking at her, his gaze running slowly over her from the top of her gleaming fair hair to the long legs bared by the happi coat. "But I'm not going to let you die, Sara. I may have lost you, but I'm not going to let him kill you. I won't lose that battle."

"Stay out of it. This isn't your battle. *I'm* not your concern any longer. Do you hear me? I want you to stay out of my—" Jordan could no longer hear her, he had closed the door behind him.

She heard the grinding of the elevator pulleys and moved automatically across the room to lock the door behind him.

She leaned against the door, her palms flat against the panels, her cheek pressed against the smooth wood. God, she was hurting. Pain was exploding through her and each breath felt like a sob. But she wasn't weeping. She wouldn't cry. It would get better. The pain would go away in time. She just had to remember how well she had gotten over him the last time. Minute by minute, hour by hour. She had to remember that magic formula. But she hadn't really known Jordan then. She hadn't realized how sweet, how endearing, how gentle he could be.

She straightened away from the door and turned to move heavily across the room. He had broken his promise and deceived her. How could she believe that the Jordan she had come to know in the last weeks wasn't a lie as well? How did she know anything connected with him was the truth?

Kemp. He wouldn't have lied about Kemp. She should be frightened but felt only numb. Strange to feel uncaring about something as important as one's own survival. Thank God, it was only temporary. As soon as this hurting stopped she would be able to think of something besides Jordan. Just as soon as the pain stopped.

Six

"Get packed." Penny strode past her into the apartment. "Now. You're getting out of this place."

Sara closed the door and locked it again. "I can't leave here. Not yet."

"You *will* leave here." Penny whirled to face Sara, her brown eyes flashing. "What kind of idealistic nitwit are you, for heaven's sake? I couldn't believe it when Jordan showed up at my office this morning and told me what was happening here."

"Jordan told you? He had no right to do that." Sara's lips tightened. "But it really doesn't make any difference. This is no one's business but my own."

"You're wrong," Penny said crisply. "It's my business and Mac's and *World Report*'s. What kind of public image do you think we'd have if you got yourself killed playing bait? And don't tell me *World*

Report isn't connected with this foolishness. How many people do you think would believe we hadn't set you up to get an exclusive?" She shook her head. "The media gets too much flack as it is without inviting this kind of trouble."

"I'll sign an affidavit clearing you of all responsibility."

"Do you think a piece of paper will make me feel better if you get your throat cut? I *am* responsible, dammit." Penny started to turn away. "I don't mind shouldering my share of responsibility, but I'm not letting anyone lay a guilt trip of that size on me. We're getting you out of San Francisco and stashing you someplace safe until they locate Kemp and can resume surveillance."

"I appreciate your position." Sara tried to keep her voice steady. Lord, this was difficult. "And I know you're my friend and concerned about me but I can't—"

"Forget about friendship." Penny turned back to face her. "That's not the primary issue here. You're an employee of *World Report* and your actions could put us in very hot water. I can't let you do that, Sara." She paused before adding deliberately, "You like your job. Is it worth giving it up to put your head on the chopping block?"

Sara's eyes widened. "You'd actually fire me?"

Penny hesitated. "Oh, hell, probably not. But Mac might not be so lenient. He was mad as hell when he heard about it. He told me very succinctly how he wanted this handled. He said 'extricate her.' Well, that's exactly what I'm doing. You're being 'extricated.' "

Sara's brow wrinkled in a frown. "This is important to me, Penny. I believe in what I'm doing. I don't know if any job is worth leaving Kemp on the streets."

"I was afraid that would be your reaction, so I took out some insurance." Penny smiled grimly. "You may be too idealistic to care about your job, but Lieutenant Blaise knuckled under quite nicely when I zeroed in on him. The police department has no desire to attract the kind of heat *World Report* can generate."

"You threatened him?"

"I told him we'd crucify him if they continued with this charade and anything happened to you. They preferred not to take the chance." Penny's tone was totally ruthless. "You'll find they now want you out of this situation as much as we do. It wouldn't surprise me if they sent a man to escort us politely to the airport to make sure you leave the city."

"Lord, you play hard ball," Sara whispered. She was experiencing a sudden surge of overwhelming relief. It was out of her hands. She was being forced to abandon Lieutenant Blaise's plan. She didn't have to wait for Kemp to come for her, for death to come for her.

"When necessary." Penny's gaze met her own. "No more arguments?"

Sara shook her head. "You appear to have closed me into a box," she said lightly. "I don't seem to have any alternative unless I choose the police escort. Where do you intend to stash me?"

"I own a tiny island off the coast of Santa Barbara." Penny made a face. "Or rather the bank and I own it. It's just a wild, hilly smudge in the middle of the ocean, but it has a nice little hacienda that was built about sixty years ago by a reclusive writer. We'll hire a helicopter from the Santa Barbara airport and I'll get you settled in at the hacienda. Then I'll come back here and watch for developments. There's no phone on the island, but when they locate Kemp I'll come back and pick you up."

"I didn't know you owned an island."

"I need a place to be by myself occasionally and I've always liked the idea of an island. Ever since I was a kid I've wanted a place that belonged only to me." She shrugged. "I guess I didn't want to share it even with my friends. This was my place. *My* sanctuary."

"But you're sharing it with me now," Sara said softly. How many other aspects of Penny's life were unknown to her? she wondered. She had assumed her friend's life was an open book, but this clearly was not the case. Penny had dreams and secrets and a past that might hold infinitely more than the career Sara had thought was her prime motivation.

"I'm sharing it because you need a sanctuary now too. Sanctuaries can be pretty wonderful when you need to hide or heal."

Sara felt a swift thrust of fresh pain. Was it so obvious that she needed healing? She tried to smile. "And what is this sanctuary called?"

"Just the island. I don't believe in giving places fancy names. It's not my style." Penny started for the bedroom. "Now, let's get you packed. Lots of sweaters and jeans. It can get chilly when the wind comes in off the sea."

The island was as wild as Penny had claimed and from the air looked even smaller. It was almost completely rockbound except for a single cove on the windward side from which a slender pier jutted out like a fragile finger into the wild surf.

"I don't see a house." Sara peered out the window of the slowly descending helicopter.

Penny nodded. "It's beyond that hill. The pines and the pepper trees are too dense to see it from here. You'll like it, I think. It took me four years of vacations to fix up the place and decorate. It's not easy to transport furniture from the mainland to the island." She grimaced. "And tradespeople are most unreasonable about delivering by boat or helicopter without charging an arm and a leg. Do you know the woman who did the window treatments actually had the nerve to charge me a penalty because she got seasick on the boat coming to the island?"

"I can understand that," Sara murmured, her gaze taking in the savage force of the waves crashing on the rocks below. "This doesn't look like the tamest surf I've ever seen."

"It isn't," Penny answered. "The currents are

treacherous around here. Riptides. So stay out of the water. Okay?"

"Okay." The helicopter had landed on the rocky edge of the shore beside the pier, and Sara looked around with interest. "I'm certainly getting a new perspective on you. Do you really like this kind of wild terrain?"

"I love it," Penny said simply. "It satisfies me." She turned to the pilot. "Wait here, Ralph. I'll be right back as soon as I help carry these groceries up to the house."

"I'll do that for you," the young pilot offered cheerfully.

"No," Penny said quickly. "Wait here. We can manage. Sara only has the one duffel bag to carry."

"I wish you could stay for a few days," Sara picked up her scarlet canvas bag, opened the heavy door, and jumped to the ground. She shivered as the sharp wind whipped around her, tearing at her hair. "I'm not sure I like the idea of being alone here."

"There's a radio and a stereo at the house." Penny got out of the helicopter and reached back into the aircraft for the sack of groceries on the floor. "And a zillion books to read. It will be good for you to relax and contemplate your navel for a few days. You may even develop a taste for the solitary life."

"I doubt it." Sara's grip tightened on the handle of her bag as she followed Penny up the winding dirt path. "It's too lonely here. I need people around me."

"I know you do." Penny gave her an affectionate glance over her shoulder. "You always were happier with conversation than a spectacular view." Her expression sobered as her gaze slid away from Sara. "I don't think you'll be lonely here."

"Then you think wrong," Sara said. "The last thing I need right now is solitude. I don't want time to—" She broke off and her steps quickened. "Are we almost there?"

"Soon." Penny turned to look at the patch of orange scarlet of the sunset filtering through the branches of the trees. "Just over the hill." She kept her gaze straight ahead. "I gather you've changed your mind about Jordan?"

Sara stiffened. "I don't want to talk about him."

"I don't either, but it's got to be done," Penny said quietly. "Because I've changed my mind about him too. I trust him, Sara."

Sara gazed at her in bewilderment. "Then you're an idiot. Lord, Penny, I never thought you'd be taken in by him too. What the devil did he say to you this morning?"

"Not much," Penny said softly. "Not much at all. But I believed every word he said. He's hurting, Sara."

"Good. He deserves to hurt." Sara swallowed to ease the painful tightness in her throat. "He lied to me. He beguiled me—"

"Beguiled." Penny's voice was thoughtful. "Good heavens, what an old-fashioned word, almost biblical. Wasn't it Lucifer who beguiled Eve in the Garden?" She grinned as she murmured softly,

" 'O why hast thou so beguiled me?' It all sounds rather enticing. Is that how you see Jordan?"

"No, I don't see—" Sara drew a shaky breath. "Look, it's stupid to talk about this. You were right and I was wrong. The volcano erupted and blew me straight to kingdom come and now I've got to pick up the pieces and go on. This isn't the time for you to play devil's advocate."

"I'm nobody's advocate. I believe in letting everyone make up his own mind, make his own decisions." Penny paused. "As I made mine. I guess I'm trying to explain why—" She stopped and appeared to be searching for words.

"Why you let him talk you into blowing Lieutenant Blaise's plan?"

"No, he didn't have to talk me into doing that." Penny hesitated again. "I was worried about leaving you here alone. You need protection." She had reached the summit of the hill and waited until Sara came even with her. "I believed him, Sara."

"You said that before. We'll have to agree to disagree."

"He gave me his word." Penny caught sight of something in the valley below. Before Sara's gaze could follow, Penny hurriedly set down the bag of groceries she was carrying. "I had to make a choice."

"What are you talking about? You're not making sense."

Penny nodded to the path leading down to the valley. "My choice."

Sara turned and felt the breath leave her body.

"No," she whispered. "You wouldn't do that to me."

Jordan was striding up the hill, the brilliant light casting a fiery glow as it tangled in the darkness of his hair. His face was shadowed but his gait was charged with the relentless energy she knew so well.

She pulled her gaze away from Jordan and turned back toward Penny. But Penny was hurrying away. "Penny!"

Penny stopped and glanced back at her. "You need protection and Jordan will make sure you get it."

"Good God, Penny, what could he have said to you that would make you do this to me?"

"He told me he'd die for you," Penny said simply. "And I think he would." Then she was gone, running down the hill toward the pier in the distance.

Sara stared after her, stunned. Penny was actually leaving her alone with Jordan. "Penny, wait!" She dropped her canvas duffel bag and darted down the hill. "You can't do this."

Penny jumped into the helicopter, slammed the door, and said something to the pilot. The helicopter lifted off, wheeling sluggishly away from the pier.

"Penny, dammit, you come back here." Sara could hear the edge of panic in her voice as she screamed the words at the top of her lungs.

Penny shook her head and blew Sara a kiss before settling back in the passenger seat.

Sara's hands clenched into fists as she watched the helicopter slowly gain altitude.

"You'd better come back to the hacienda with me now. The wind is sharp here on the shore."

Jordan's voice was quiet, almost soft behind her, but she stiffened as if struck by a bullet.

She turned slowly to face him. "How did you do it?"

"You mean convince your friend that I was sincere?" His smile was bittersweet. "I told you once that she was very perceptive. She has your best interests at heart and doesn't give a damn whom she uses to serve them. I assure you I didn't try to con her."

"You don't have to try; it's second nature to you."

He flinched. "I know better than to argue with you. You wouldn't believe me anyway."

"No." Her nails bit into her palms. "I'm glad you realize that."

"Oh, I do." He met her gaze steadily. "I have no delusions either about the way you feel about me or about what I've done. I accept the responsibility for both."

"Then suppose you phone the mainland and get Penny to send a helicopter to pick me up. I'm not staying here."

He shook his head. "There's no telephone."

Penny had mentioned that, Sara remembered now. "This is crazy! I won't stay here alone with you, Jordan."

"We won't be alone. Cam's rented a launch and will be here tomorrow morning with supplies."

"Cam! He's in on this madness too?"

"Perhaps he's more like me than you thought. At least, he understands and can empathize." He jammed his hands in the pockets of his denim jacket. "Or maybe you think I conned him too. You seem to think I have the eloquence of Lucifer."

Sara had a fleeting memory of Penny's words regarding the beguiling of Eve. "The comparison isn't inappropriate, but eloquence is effective only if one is willing to listen. I gave up listening to you when that phone rang last night."

"I know. That's why I went to your friend Penny. You had to be gotten out of that trap, and if I couldn't do it, I wasn't above using anyone who could." The corners of his lips lifted in a mirthless smile. "Which, of course, substantiates your opinion of my character. But it doesn't matter what you think of me. The only thing that matters is that you're safe here and I'm going to make sure you stay that way." He turned away. "I'm going back to the house to start dinner. Come when you're ready."

He walked away from her and a moment later was climbing the hill. Sara gazed at his back, feeling the anger and frustration bubbling through her in a hot stream. "It's not going to be that easy," she called after him. "I'll be damned if I'll let you do this to me. I won't be under your thumb ever again."

He turned to face her, his expression reflecting only an immense weariness. "For heaven's sake, do you think Penny would go along with this without exacting promises? I told her I wouldn't coerce you in any way. I'll make the same promise to you, if you'll believe me."

"I won't believe you."

"I didn't think so." His expression hardened. "I guess that doesn't matter either." He paused and then burst out, "Hell, yes, it matters, but I can live with it. I can stand anything if it keeps you alive. You're not leaving this island until Kemp is no longer a danger to you, and I'm going to be closer than your shadow while you're here."

"The hell you will."

He nodded. "It will probably be pretty close to hell for both of us." He turned and once more began climbing the hill, his long-legged stride swiftly covering the distance to the summit. For a moment his slender, powerful body was silhouetted against the sullen scarlet of the sky, then he disappeared from view as he started down the other side of the hill.

Sara stood there, feeling very much alone. The wind's bite seemed suddenly keener, the pounding of the waves against the rocks wilder. She turned and looked out toward the sea. She felt as savage as the elements at this moment. If Penny had been here, she would have been tempted to strangle her, she thought grimly. How had Penny dared to put her in this position? Both Jordan and Penny had treated her like a puppet.

Well, she was no puppet and she would stack her mental abilities against theirs any day. Her only weakness had been trust in both of them, a trust they had blown to smithereens. Jordan had told her that her loss of trust in him had freed him, but she didn't feel free. She felt heartsick and lonely and empty inside. She would get over it. She would learn to be as tough as Penny and Jordan. She would stay here for a while and watch the turbulence of the sea and try to banish the storm within herself and compose herself to face Jordan again.

The spicy aroma of onions and peppers greeted her as soon as she walked into the red-tiled hacienda and she followed the fragrance down the terrazzo hall to the back of the house. Jordan glanced up from stirring the mixture in the frying pan. "I put your suitcase upstairs in the master bedroom." He smiled faintly. "It not much bigger than the other two, but it has a private bath. Dinner will be ready in fifteen minutes."

"I'm not giving in, you know."

"I know."

"But I'm not stupid enough to spend the night outside just to avoid you."

"Very sensible of you."

"I'm going to get off this island."

He resumed stirring the onion and peppers. "When it's safe."

"No, I won't be treated like an idiot child. I don't know what made you and Penny think I'd be malleable enough to let you get away with this but—"

"Not malleable." He looked down at the pan. "Trusting. I told you once you were too trusting. Even when you thought I'd betrayed you, you still had to trust someone. You always will, Sara."

"No," she said sharply. "I've learned my lesson. I'll be just as tough and cynical as you and Penny."

"No, you won't." He looked up, his expression grave. "You'd like to believe you can change, but it won't happen. You're gentle and loving and strong enough not to let people like me twist you or make you into something you aren't."

"I'm not so sure I want to be gentle or loving any longer."

"You do. I'm sure enough for both of us." He set the frying pan on the back burner. "I'm making a casserole. If you like, I'll fix a tray and bring it up to you. I can understand why you'd think it best not to be around me."

"I told you I had no reason to avoid you," she said curtly. "I'll come down after I've showered and changed." She started to turn away.

"There will be plenty of reason to avoid me tonight."

She quickly glanced back over her shoulder.

A flicker of humor indented the corners of his lips. "Don't look so wary." He turned away. "I was talking about the onions. I'm crazy about them, remember?"

Seven

"I've never seen you like this." Sara pushed away her plate and studied Jordan's face across the kitchen table. "Is this another act?"

Jordan shook his head. "All the acts are over and the curtain has officially rung down." He stood up. "Have you finished? I'll get the coffee."

Sara watched him cross the kitchen, a puzzled frown wrinkling her brow. There was something different about Jordan tonight. The stillness that was so much a part of him was still present, his strength of will was more than evident, yet there was something missing. Suddenly she realized what was out of kilter. The underlying tension that had always charged his every action was gone. "You're . . . relaxed."

He turned away from the cabinet, the coffee carafe in hand, and returned to the table. "Am I?"

He poured the steaming coffee into her cup. "I don't feel that way, but then, I don't suppose you've ever seen me when I wasn't desperate. You're right, I've been onstage since the day I met you."

"Desperate," she repeated. "That's a strange term to use."

"It's even worse than strange to experience; it's damn uncomfortable." He poured his own coffee and set the carafe on the table before resuming his seat. He leaned back in his chair and stretched his long legs out before him. "You've never been desperate, have you, Sara?"

She thought about it. "No, I guess I haven't." She had been deeply unhappy, even desolate, but had never known the sharp edge of desperation. "I didn't think you'd ever be desperate about anything. You've always been very much in control." Her lips tightened. "Of everything and everyone."

He lifted his cup to his lips. "Control was important to me. It was the only way I could keep my world from shattering into a million pieces. I couldn't let that happen."

"You're speaking in that past tense but you're still trying to control me. What do you call stranding me on this island and not letting me leave?"

"The last hurrah?" He lifted his cup in a self-mocking toast. "Or perhaps a chance to save my sanity. What do you call it?"

"Arrogance." She stood up. "I don't want any coffee. I think I'll go to bed. Tomorrow when Cam gets here I'm leaving the island. If he won't take me back himself, I'm sure there'll be a radio on the launch he'll let me use. But I can't believe he'll really go along with you."

"If he doesn't, he won't stay long, and you'll be left with the wicked seducer. I'm sure you don't want that to come to pass."

"You appear to find this amusing. Well, I don't."

"Oh, not amusing. I've never been fond of black comedy." He slowly rose to his feet. "But perhaps I do see a certain dry irony in the situation. You've always wanted to see me stripped of all my protective barriers, and now, when it doesn't matter any longer, I can let you see me as I am. Don't you find that a bit bizarre?"

"I'm afraid I don't enjoy twisted humor."

"I know you don't. It's too dark for you. *I'm* too dark for you. I always knew that." He put his cup down in the saucer and smiled faintly. "But you didn't. I think my darkness attracted you. You wanted to light up all my hidden corners. I was a challenge to you."

"No," she protested, shocked. "It wasn't like that, I loved— I was infatuated with you."

"Were you? Think about it. All your life people have loved you. You told me that until the very moment your parents died you had a wonderful relationship with them. You've always had good friends and you're beautifully uncomplicated emotionally." He paused and when he spoke again his voice had thickened. "Very beautifully. Then I appeared in your life and I was different. No one in her right mind would call me uncomplicated, and I couldn't give you any of the nice tidy responses you were accustomed to receiving. I deluged you, drowned you with what I felt for you, but I also excited you. You were ready for something different and I gave it to you. You wanted a challenge and I gave that to you too. You might remember those things when you're cursing me for making you into a victim."

Was he right? Sara wondered uncertainly. She had always had a passion for probing beneath the surface and Jordan had presented her with a fascinating enigma. Had she instinctively responded to that challenge and gone after what she wanted with a ruthlessness as great as the one she had accused him of possessing? "Are you saying I used you?"

"Not intentionally."

She nibbled worriedly at her lower lip. "You have to be wrong. I've never used anyone."

He was silent, gazing at her steadily.

"I *hate* users."

"Don't fret, Sara." Jordan's tone was gentle. "I didn't mind being used. I was willing to let you use me in any way you needed me. It was worth it to me."

She shook her head, backing away from him. "But I've never—" She swallowed hard. "Jordan, I'm not a user."

"We all use each other. The only crime is in using and not letting yourself be used in return. You always gave more than you took, Sara."

But she hadn't realized that she had been taking anything at all. Now she found herself wondering how much Jordan had feigned possessiveness to give her something "different." He knew her so well that it was possible he had seen something in her character that had remained unknown to her until he had ripped aside the veil. "Why didn't you say something to me before? Why did you take all the blame on yourself?"

"Because the fault was mine," he said simply. "Just because your motives weren't quite as idealistic as you thought doesn't make you guilty. I did everything you accused me of doing and, once I figured out what drew you to me, I used that too."

But she had been guilty, too, she was beginning to realize. She had been so absorbed in trying to unravel the puzzle that was Jordan Bandor that it was possible she had been blind to her own selfishness.

"Don't worry about it," Jordan said gently. "It's all water under the bridge now. Go to bed and get some sleep." He smiled crookedly. "I didn't let you rest very much last night, did I?"

Sara could feel the color sting her cheeks as memories flooded back to her, piercing her confusion with hot arrows of sensuality. The firelight flickering over Jordan's naked body as he moved within her. His face dark, intense, above her, drawn taut with a pleasure that was close to pain. She could feel her breasts swell beneath her oversize sweater as heat began to build within her. Her gaze unconsciously moved over him, taking in the strength, the sheer maleness of him. She abruptly realized what was happening to her and jerked her gaze away. Not again, she wouldn't be caught again. How did she know this new facet Jordan was presenting to her wasn't as false as the other ones? She turned away. "I'll rest very well tonight. Good night, Jordan."

"I hope you're right." He turned and started to stack the dishes on the table. "You can try anyway."

"I'll go to sleep right away," she stated flatly. She left the kitchen and started down the hall.

But she didn't go to sleep right away. It was almost dawn before she was able to bridle the emotions and possibilities Jordan had raised, so that she could drop into a troubled sleep.

"Sorry, luv, I can't help you," Cam said gently. "Not this time."

"I don't believe it." Sara gazed from Cam to Jordan and then back again. "You're actually going to help him? There are laws against things like this."

"No crime has been committed," Jordan said quietly. "You came here of your own free will with the intention of staying for some time. Just because you've changed your mind doesn't obligate Cam or me to furnish you with the means to leave."

She turned to Cam. "But I don't want to stay—" She broke off. Cam's expression was sympathetic but every bit as determined as Jordan's. Her frustration and anger were escalating by the second. "I thought you'd help me."

Cam shrugged. "He's my brother and he believes what he's doing is right. He honestly wants what's best for you, Sara."

"My Lord, how chauvinistic can you get?" Her hands closed into fists at her sides. "I'm the one to decide what's best for me."

Neither man answered her.

Her anger flared to a new high. "Damn you," she said through her teeth. "Damn you both." She turned and ran from the room. She found herself dashing down the hall and then outside. Fog suddenly surrounded her and a cold, damp wind whipped her face as she ran up the rocky dirt path leading to the top of the hill.

"Sara!" It was Jordan's voice behind her but she ignored it. "Sara, dammit, stop. You can't make it to the launch before I—" He broke off but she heard the pounding of his steps on the stony path behind her.

The launch! She'd had no plan in mind when she ran out of the house. She'd just wanted to get away from Jordan and Cam before she did something violent. But if she could reach Cam's launch . . . Even if the keys weren't in the ignition, she could use the radio to call the mainland. A burst of adrenaline lent speed to her feet as she flew down the other side of the hill. She saw the sleek white launch anchored at the pier and her heart leapt with hope.

"Sara, don't—"

The stones beneath the leather soles of her boots were slick and she slipped and then regained her balance and kept running. He was closer. She could hear the sound of his harsh, rough breathing behind her.

She had reached the shore and the stones were even slicker next to the water. She was going too fast to stop. She lost her footing and fell sidewise, struggling desperately to gain her balance.

Pain exploded in her temple. Blinding pain. Darkness came and went like the cold mists around her.

"Sara." Jordan's face above her was as agonized as his voice. "Oh, God, Sara. Don't be hurt. Tell me you're not hurt."

Why was he saying something so idiotic when he could clearly see she *was* hurt! "My head."

Jordan's face was spinning, dissolving. How strange and magical. But he was a magician, she remembered dimly. He could transform himself at will, and weave spells that enthralled and beguiled. *Beguiled.* That biblical word again. Penny had said something about—

"Talk to me." Jordan's voice was urgent, frantic, as his hands ran over her arms and legs. "Where does it hurt?"

"Only my head." Her eyes closed. "I'm dizzy."

"Don't go to sleep. Do you hear me? You've got to stay awake."

His tone was so commanding, she felt as if he were keeping her conscious by sheer willpower alone. Perhaps he was. She didn't seem to have much will of her own at present.

"Say something. Recite poetry. Anything."

How peculiarly he was behaving. Why would he want her to do anything so idiotic as recite poetry. "I can't think of any poetry now."

"Then recite the Pledge of Allegiance or the Bill of Rights. All of you Yanks memorize those things, right? Come on, open your eyes and talk to me."

She slowly opened her eyes. His face was close to her own. Jordan had such a powerful, fascinating face, a face that filled her world. Why hadn't she realized that before? Why was she fighting him, when the tie that bound them together was so much stronger than what was tearing them apart? She vaguely remembered it had something to do with what had happened in the past, but she was too tired to think now. Perhaps tomorrow . . .

"No! Stay with me. Say something to me."

It was terribly hard to stay with him, and what could she say? She couldn't remember that blasted Pledge of Allegiance either. All she could recall were the words Penny had quoted. Perhaps he'd be happy with that. "Oh why hast thou so beguiled me?"

He inhaled sharply. "God, love, I never meant . . ."

What was he talking about? She had hurt him in some way and she had to try to . . . The mists were closing in and she tried desperately to push them away. Jordan needed her.

His hands were gripping her shoulders as if to forcibly keep her with him. "No, don't close your eyes! Please, Sara."

She heard no more.

•　　•　　•

She opened her eyes to see Cam smiling down at her. "It's about time you came back to us. Four more hours and I would have had another patient. Jordan is practically a basket case. He was afraid you'd gone into a coma."

Sara lifted her hand to her throbbing temple. Running. She had been running. The stones had been so slick. "I fell."

"You bet you did." Cam dropped down into the easy chair beside the bed. "And gave yourself one hell of a whack. You've been unconscious for the last few hours." He patted her hand. "Don't worry. The doctor said you had only a slight concussion. You're to stay in bed and take it easy for the next twenty-four hours, but after that you should be fine."

"Doctor?" She sat up, flinching as a jagged pain ripped through her head. "What doctor?"

"Jordan had me radio for a doctor to be flown in from the mainland to examine you. Dr. Molsen just left. Jordan is walking down to the helicopter with him." Cam made a face. "I don't think Jordan believed him when he said you'd regain consciousness any minute and intends to cross-examine the poor bastard. How do you feel?"

"Like I have a king-size hangover."

"How would you know how that feels?" Cam's dark eyes were twinkling. "I've never even seen you tipsy."

"I've sowed a few wild oats like everyone else. Once when I was in college I remember waking up and being in such pain even the sheet covering me hurt and—" She broke off as another pain knifed through her head. She fell back against the pillows and closed her eyes. "That's when I learned the value of moderation in all things."

"You miss a lot of fun that way. Personally, I'm in favor of indulging myself with a little excess every now and then." A cold cloth was laid on her forehead and Sara sighed with relief as Cam wiped her face with almost maternal gentleness. "Better?"

She didn't dare risk nodding her head. "Yes."

"The doctor gave you a shot for pain and left you some pills to take later tonight." Cam continued to move the cloth over her face. "You're going to be fine, luv. Just put up with all this bother a little longer and we'll have you on your feet again in no time." For a few moments there was a silence in the room as soothing as the stroking of Cam's touch before a distant chugging of the rotors of a helicopter broke the tranquility. "There goes the doctor. That means Jordan should be back pretty soon."

Jordan. Sara's muscles suddenly stiffened and the soothing motion of Cam's hand paused. "Relax. No one's going to hassle you. Jordan's probably in worse shape than you are."

"I doubt it," she said dryly. "I'm the one who feels like every sound is setting off an explosion in my head."

"Then I'd better shut up." He paused. "Just one more thing, Sara. Don't blame Jordan too much for what happened, will you? I guarantee he's blaming himself enough for the two of you."

"I don't blame Jordan for my fall," she said wearily. "It was an accident and could have happened even if I hadn't been running away from him. I have enough counts against him without blaming him for that too." She turned her head away. "I don't want to talk about Jordan. It gives me even more of a headache than that fall I took. I'm going to go back to sleep."

"Good idea," Cam said softly. "The great bard said that 'sleep brings counsel.' I think we could all use a little counseling. There has to be some solution to this mess."

"Does there? I don't know . . ."

The room was in almost total darkness when she opened her eyes again, and she could only vaguely discern the figure sitting in the chair by the bed. "Cam?" she asked drowsily.

"No." Jordan leaned forward. "Are you all right? Do you need something?"

"Water. My throat is dry." She sat up in bed and found to her relief that her headache had faded to a dull throb behind her eyes. "I can get it."

"Sit still." Jordan's voice was hoarse. He switched on the lamp on the bedside table and poured a half glass of water from the thermos carafe on the table. "Do you need a pain pill?"

"No, I don't think so." She took the glass of water and drank it thirstily. "I don't like to take strong sedatives unless—" She broke off as her gaze lifted to his face. "You're the one who looks as though he should take something."

Jordan looked ravaged . . . empty. She experienced a swift rush of sympathy and hurriedly lowered her gaze so that he wouldn't be aware of that brief moment of weakness. "Why don't you go to bed? I don't need you."

His smile was a mere stretching of lips as he took the empty glass and set it on the bedside table. "I know you don't. But I need to be here. I promise you that I won't bother you. I'll just sit here and watch over you. Okay?"

She frowned. "No, it's not okay. I'm fine and I certainly don't need or want anyone holding a watch over me. Go to bed."

He stood there, looking at her for a long moment. Then to her surprise he turned away. "All right, I'll leave you alone. God knows, I can't blame you for wanting to see the last of me." He switched off the lamp. "Call if you need anything."

She watched him move toward the door, a solid silhouette in the darkness. It wasn't like Jordan to give up so easily and it gave her a twinge of uneasiness. "Jordan."

"Yes."

"Cam said you were blaming yourself for my injury," she said haltingly. "I just wanted you to know that I realize you never intended to hurt me."

"That's very kind of you." His words were oddly muffled. "But it was entirely my fault that it happened."

For some reason she wanted desperately to comfort him. Where had her anger and bitterness gone?

He opened the door, and for an instant he was framed against the dimly lighted hallway. He was standing very straight, the line of his spine taut as if to withstand the force of a blow. The door closed behind him.

So much pain. Even though he had left the room she could feel the waves of agony that had radiated from him encompass her. She could feel them as if it were her own pain, as if in some mysterious fashion they were joined.

She had a vague memory of thinking something like that after she had been hurt. There had been a warmth, a certainty, a bonding.

And a realization.

Sara slowly lay back down but not to sleep. She was too alert, too electrified by the stunning knowledge that had come to her. She would have to think, to come to terms with that discovery.

And then she must come to a decision.

Cam rose from the couch and came forward as soon as he heard Jordan's footsteps on the stairs. His gaze searched his brother's face. "She's awake?"

Jordan nodded jerkily. "She seems okay." He smiled bitterly. "As well as could be expected after a blow on the head like that."

"It was an accident," Cam said gently. "You speak as if you struck her with a blackjack."

"The result was the same. I could have killed her. God, I hoped this time it would be different. I hoped I could keep her safe."

"It is different." Cam took an impulsive step forward. "Forget Bandora. If there was any guilt there, it was your father's and not yours."

"No, I was to blame then too. Just as I am now."

"Jordan, dammit, you can't—" Cam broke off. He had fought this battle before and had never been able to convince Jordan. He should have known he'd be even more bullheaded on the subject after Sara's injury. "You're wrong and someday I'm going to make you see it."

Jordan shook his head. "Thanks for trying, Cam." He descended the last three steps and started across the hall toward the front door. "I'm going for a walk."

Cam looked at him in surprise. "In the middle of the night?"

"I need to *do* something." Jordan jerked the door open. "Anything. Stay awake in case Sara needs something, will you?" He smiled mirthlessly. "She'd probably have a relapse if I went back into her room. She made it clear she didn't want me there. Who the hell can blame her?"

"I'll watch her. Be careful if you go down to the shore. We don't want another casualty."

"It would be no great loss." He glanced over his shoulder and smiled bitterly. "But don't worry,

I'm one of the destroyers of the world, not one of the victims."

"That's a bunch of bull."

"Is it? Look at the record."

Eight

"You must be feeling better." Cam smiled with pleasure as he watched Sara coming down the stairs. "That's terrific. No more headache?"

Sara shook her head. "I feel fine. Where's Jordan?"

A flicker of surprise crossed Cam's face. "Now, that's a question I didn't expect. Do you want to know because you want to see him or because you want to avoid him?"

"I want to see him," Sara said crisply. "Right now. Where is he?"

"Down at the launch. He's arranging a phone patch up to Penny Lassiter's apartment in San Francisco." Cam frowned. "Look, Jordan's feeling pretty rough this morning. If you're planning on mounting a full-scale attack, can't it wait until—"

"Why is he feeling rough?" Sara interrupted. "His reaction to this accident has definitely been on the extreme side."

Cam hesitated. "Jordan is complicated."

"So he told me. He thinks that was why I was attracted to him."

"Was it?"

A sudden smile lit her face. "Perhaps. In the beginning."

"But not now?"

"Oh, no," she said softly. "Not now."

Cam's face narrowed on her face, noting the faint flush coloring her cheeks and the brilliant sparkling of her eyes. "You're not angry any longer. Maybe sleep did bring counsel after all?"

"I did some thinking." She turned toward the door. "And made a few decisions."

"Sara."

She glanced back at him and was surprised to see his expression was troubled. "What's wrong?"

"You're going to try to work out your problems with Jordan, aren't you?"

"Why the long face? I thought that's what you wanted."

"I do." He hesitated. "It's just that it may be too late."

She felt a swift thrust of fear. "What do you mean?"

"There's a hell of a lot you don't know about Jordan," he said quietly. "And this accident triggered something pretty traumatic in him."

"The reason I don't know as much as I should about Jordan is because no one will tell me," Sara said with exasperation. "He's always been a bloody mystery man and I'm getting pretty tired of running into walls wherever I go. Will you please spit out what you mean instead of giving me these blasted hints."

"I can't do that. I wasn't at Bandora when it happened and what Jordan told me later was in strict confidence."

"For heaven's sake, I'm his wife, Cam."

Cam shook his head stubbornly. "I promised. You'll have to ask him."

"You're just as obstinate as he is." She strode toward the door and flung it open. "I will ask him and I'll get a few answers too."

"I hope so," Cam murmured as the door swung shut behind her. "Lord, I hope so, luv."

"Jordan." Sara moistened her dry lips with her tongue. Damn, she was nervous. She had been filled with such optimism and joy when she had opened her eyes this morning and now Cam's words had robbed her of both. She took a step closer to the launch and called again, "Jordan. It's Sara."

Jordan stepped out of the cabin and stood looking at her. "What are you doing out of bed? Dammit, you're not even wearing a coat. Are you trying to catch pneumonia?" He tore off his blue-jean jacket as he strode across the deck and down the gangplank. He draped the jacket over her shoulders, thrusting her right arm in the sleeve. "If you wanted to see me, why couldn't you have sent Cam down?" He thrust her left arm in the other sleeve and began to button the jacket. "Or maybe you wanted to make a try for the launch again? I won't let you leave, Sara. There's no way—"

"Will you please be quiet," she asked crossly. "In the first place, I don't need this damn jacket. The sweater I'm wearing is thick enough to keep an Eskimo warm." She was more than warm, she realized breathlessly. He was only a half step away and the scent of soap and his aftershave was enveloping her. The top button of his blue chambray shirt was undone and she could glimpse the dark hair that thatched his chest. She had a sudden urge to touch him, to wind her fingers in the soft springiness of his hair. She jerked her gaze back to his face and tried to remember what she'd been saying. "Cam said the doctor told you I'd be back to normal in twenty-four hours, and he was right. I feel fine." He started to speak, but she put her fingers over his lips to silence him. "And I didn't come down to hijack the launch either. Now that we've disposed of all that foolishness, may I tell you why I did come?"

He didn't answer. She realized her fingers on his lips were trembling, the flesh tingling as his warm breath touched her like a kiss. Her hand dropped to her side and she laughed shakily. "Did you manage to patch into Penny's line?"

"Cam told you?" He looked away from her. "Not yet, but the phone company is working on it. It won't do you any good. Either Cam or I will be manning the radio all the time. You're not going to be able to send an SOS."

"Did I say I wanted to send a message? It would hardly do me any good to contact Penny. I think she's demonstrated who's corner she's in on this matter." She thrust her hands into the pockets of the jean jacket. "Now, will you please listen to me?"

"I'm listening." He still wasn't looking at her. "Say what you want and get back to the house, where it's warm."

"I told you—" She stopped. He thought he was in for some kind of tirade, she realized suddenly. Every muscle of his body was taut and braced to resist it. Tenderness swept through her. "I'm not going to try to leave the island, Jordan."

If anything, his tension increased. "Sure."

"I mean it. Dammit, Jordan, look at me."

His gaze reluctantly moved to her face. "This isn't a game, Sara. I'll let you go as soon as it's safe for you but don't try—"

"Hush." She cupped his face in her hands. "You couldn't force me to leave. I'm staying. Is that clear?"

"No." His face was expressionless. "It's not at all clear."

"Then I'll try to be more explicit." She drew a deep breath. She shouldn't have touched him. Heat was spiraling through her and she wanted to get the words over with so that she could move into his arms. If he still wanted her. Oh, Lord, what if he didn't want her now? Jordan's face held no emotion whatever and Cam had been so damn negative. "I want to try living together again.

I've been thinking and—" She stopped. This was even harder than she had imagined it would be.

Jordan's expression remained unrevealing, but she could feel the shock that rippled through his body. "Why?"

"I think we could make our marriage work."

He smiled crookedly. "Where have I heard that before?"

"There were so many things I didn't understand," she whispered. "About you and about myself. I still have a great deal to learn, but I'm on the right road."

He took a step back and her hands fell away from his face. "No." His voice held a note of violence. "You don't know what you're saying. You're on some kind of guilt trip because you've suddenly realized you're not quite the martyr you thought you were. Now you think I'm the martyr and you should give the poor bastard another chance."

"I don't think you're a martyr." She was trying to hold on to her patience. "But at the moment I think you're a stubborn idiot. Listen closely, Jordan, I do feel guilty but not guilty enough to come back and live with you to make some kind of compensation. I *would* have to have a king-size martyr complex to do something like that."

"Not necessarily. You still want me physically and that would sweeten the pill."

She should have known Jordan would pick up the signals she was sending, she thought ruefully. "Yes, it would sweeten it for both of us, wouldn't it?" He didn't answer and she felt a tiny flutter of panic. "Or maybe you don't feel the same way. Don't you want me anymore, Jordan?"

A betraying muscle jerked in his cheek. "You know better than that," he said hoarsely. "I'm so hard right now, it's killing me. I want you all the time. It's like a fever."

"And you're a fever in my blood, too," she said softly, taking a step toward him "But there's more than that between us. You once tried to tell me that, but the sex was so strong it seemed to over-shadow everything else and I couldn't see what it was hiding."

"And you think you see now?"

She took another step nearer. "I don't think—I know. I realized last night that no matter how many problems there are to overcome living with you, it's better than living without you." She smiled shakily. "It's amazing how that knock on the head seemed to jar everything into place."

His face paled. "Don't joke. I almost killed you."

"You didn't do any such thing." She frowned. "It was an accident. I slipped on the stones, dammit."

He turned away. "Go back to the house." He strode across the pier and up the gangplank. "Did Cam fix you any breakfast?"

"Breakfast?" She gazed at him, stunned. "If I'd wanted breakfast, I would have fixed it myself. I needed to talk to you. Where the hell are you going?"

"We've talked," he said curtly. "There's nothing more to say."

"You stop right there, Jordan Bandor." Her voice was trembling. "I need an answer and you're going to give me one."

He stopped but didn't turn around. "I gave you an answer."

Pain. She couldn't believe there could be this much pain. "No?"

"No."

She swallowed. "Why?"

"I told you I'd never risk—" He broke off. "Go tell Cam to give you some breakfast." Without another word he disappeared into the cabin.

He hadn't really said he didn't love her, and he did want her. She grabbed at the realization with a desperation born of panic. He had said only that he was afraid to risk. Risk what? she wondered in frustration. She took an impulsive step toward the launch and then stopped. It was no use going after Jordan when she had no ammunition with which to fight him. But she'd get that ammunition, blast it. This nonsense had to stop.

She whirled on her heel and strode down the pier and across the rocky shore. A moment later she was swiftly climbing the hill toward the hacienda.

The front door flew open with such force it crashed against the wall. Cam looked up in surprise from the magazine he was flipping through as Sara marched into the room. His lips pursed in a soundless whistle as his gaze fastened on her stormy face. "Problems?"

"You're damn right there are problems." Sara slammed the door behind her, strode over to the couch across from the armchair in which Cam was sitting, and plopped down. "What else can you expect when the world is populated with stubborn, idiotic men? But I've had enough of it. You're going to tell me what I need to know if I have to strangle it out of you."

"My, my, how violent we're being," Cam said as he tossed the magazine on the occasional table beside his chair. "I gather Jordan was uncooperative."

"Jordan was as stubborn as you are. He won't talk to me." She found herself blinking back tears. "It hurts, Cam. Maybe I deserve it, but it still hurts."

"You don't deserve it." Cam's dark eyes were warm with sympathy. "Neither of you deserves it."

"Then talk to me," Sara said. "What happened at Bandora?"

"I promised I wouldn't—" Cam stopped, his gaze resting on Sara's face. "Oh, stop looking at me like that. I feel as if I've kicked a koala." A sudden smile lit his face. "I guess I can always claim you coerced me. After all, you did threaten to strangle me."

Sara straightened and leaned forward. "I need to know, Cam."

"I think you do," Cam said quietly. "What do you want me to tell you?"

"You said Jordan was scared. What is he afraid of?"

"Death," Cam said quietly. "Oh, not for himself. I think he's afraid of killing you."

Her eyes widened in shock. "That's crazy. He practically wrapped me in cotton during the time we lived together. I could scarcely breathe much less . . ." She stopped as understanding suddenly dawned. "Sweet heaven, that's it, isn't it?"

Cam nodded slowly. "He built you a nice mink-lined cage to keep you safe, to keep you from wandering away from him to a place where he couldn't protect you. He *has* to protect you, Sara. It's a compulsion that goes way back."

"Back to Bandora?"

He hesitated before nodding again. "Back to Bandora. How much do you know about Bandora?"

"Not much. Jordan only said he and his father loved the place."

"The station was an obsession with Jordan's father, and he raised Jordan to feel the same way about it." Cam looked down at the bold stripes of the area rug. "The outback can be pretty cruel and godawful lonely. You either love it or hate it. Jordan and his father loved it. Jordan's mother hated it." He shrugged. "Who could blame her? She was a city girl from Adelaide and Jordan's father left her alone on the property a good portion of the time when he started organizing the tourist expeditions into the outback. From the time Jordan was a small child, his father dominated his life. His father and Bandora. Not that Jordan didn't love his mother, there just didn't seem room for her."

Sara shivered. "How terrible it must have been for her. No one to talk to. She must have been so lonely."

"Yes, she was lonely and unhappy." Cam paused. "Terribly unhappy. But it was Jordan's father who was at fault. Not Jordan."

"Of course not. He was only a child."

"Jordan doesn't see it that way. He thinks he should have realized how unhappy she was. He thinks he should have been able to read the signs and prevented it. He told me if he'd only studied her, got to know how she thought and reacted, he might have been able to save her."

Sara's hand closed on the arm of the couch. "Save her?"

Cam lifted his gaze to meet her own. "Three days before Jordan and his father were due back from an expedition, she drove a jeep into the outback and didn't come back. The search party found her body in the jeep seven days later. She hadn't taken any water with her and she'd died of heat stroke and thirst."

"Oh, no," Sara whispered. "Could it have been an accident?"

Cam shook his head. "She left a note in her bedroom at the station to say good-bye."

Jordan had been only twelve at the time, Sara remembered. She felt sick as she thought of how he must have felt, the guilt and despair that must have scarred him. "It must have been a nightmare for him."

Cam nodded. "He nearly went crazy when they found the body. Death by thirst isn't pleasant."

"His father took him along?" Sara asked in horror.

"He was considered a man on Bandora." His lips tightened. "He ran away from the jeep and didn't come back to the station for over a week. He never told anyone where he had gone or what had happened to him during the week, but somewhere along the way his left eye had been terribly damaged and was infected. The doctors couldn't save it."

"But he was only a child," Sara protested, fighting back the tears. "They should never have let him see his mother. Someone should have stopped them."

"Jordan's father was a hard man," Cam said. "And he raised Jordan in a hard school. I don't think he even realized his mother's death would affect Jordan any different than it did him."

"How did it affect his father?"

"He found it convenient to believe his wife was 'unbalanced.' He married my mother a year later." His lips twisted. "Of course, she had enough money to soothe his grief by making Bandora into the kind of showplace he'd always dreamed."

"Delightful."

"But it was too late for Jordan. He couldn't stand living at Bandora any longer. We were both sent away to school in Melbourne and then traveled for a while. When Jordan's father died, my mother returned to Marasef and Jordan sold Bandora. We formed Bandora Enterprises and bought our first hotel in Sydney. Four years later Jordan bought Half Moon Bay." Cam leaned back in his chair. "There it is. Does it help, luv?"

"Yes." Her eyes were still glinting with tears. "But it would have helped more if someone had told me all this when I first met Jordan. I would have understood so much." Jordan's possessiveness, his watchfulness, his obsession with keeping her safe. She stood up. "But better late than not at all. Thank you, Cam."

He rose to his feet and inclined his head. "My pleasure. But remember, you threatened me with dire and bloody consequences to squeeze all this out of me."

"I'll remember. Will you do me another favor?"

He looked at her quizzically.

"Go down to the pier and persuade Jordan to come back to the house. I want to talk to him." She made a rueful face. "And he's made it quite clear he doesn't want any further conversation with me."

"This is very hard for him."

"That's his fault," she said as she turned and walked briskly toward the stairs. "I'm doing my best to simplify things. If he doesn't start cooperating, I'll make sure he's going to find it gets a heck of a lot harder."

Cam looked startled, and then an impish grin touched his lips. "You know, I bet you will." He began whistling softly as he strolled toward the front door.

•   •   •

The knock on her bedroom door was perfunctory before the door swung open and Jordan entered. "Cam said you weren't feeling well. I told you that you should have stayed in bed, dammit. Should I radio for the doctor?"

"I'm feeling fine." Sara turned away from the window to face him. "I just wanted to see you."

He stopped, his expression wary. "I think I may have a bone to pick with Cam. He scared the hell out of me."

"It wasn't Cam's fault. I asked him to get you up here. I was afraid you wouldn't come if I asked you." She smiled. "And I thought it only fair to give you another chance to come to your senses before I start my campaign."

He scowled. "I don't know what the devil you're talking about."

"You will," she said serenely. "But first, the offer. Will you let me come back to you so that we can make a stab at living in connubial bliss?"

His jaw squared as his teeth clenched. "I can't."

"You'll find that you can." She smiled sunnily at him. "But I can understand why you're having problems with this. One more question, and this is the big one. Do you love me?"

He was silent, gazing at her, his face twisted in torment.

"Do you?"

"Yes," he finally said thickly. "God, yes, I love you."

"Good." She released her breath in a rush of relief. She hadn't realized she'd been holding it. "That makes it easier."

"No, it doesn't. I almost killed you," Jordan said harshly. "This mess with Kemp would never have happened if I hadn't driven you away from me. And then, when I tried to put things right, I almost killed you. You were within an inch of falling into the sea. I won't take that risk again."

"You're not thinking clearly." She smiled at him lovingly. "I never realized how thickheaded you could be. I guess I'll just have to blow in a little fresh air to clear the cobwebs."

He started to turn away.

"Jordan." Her voice was very gentle. "I'm not your mother."

He froze. "Cam appears to have a very big mouth."

"You should have told me yourself."

He didn't look at her. "What could I have told you? That I killed my own mother?"

"You didn't kill her. She killed herself."

"No, I should have known. I should have been able to see—"

"You weren't responsible for her death," Sara interrupted firmly. "Adults are accountable for their own actions. She could have left your father and built a new life for herself."

"Like you did?" he asked bitterly. "And then I followed you and nearly—"

"Jordan!" Sara gazed at him, tenderness and exasperation battling within her. "I'm *glad* you followed me. I would have been incomplete for the rest of my life if you hadn't."

He started for the door. "You always did have a

soft heart, but pity's getting in the way of your sense of self-preservation."

"An you obviously have a very soft head," she said with frustration. "There's no pity involved here. I *love* you."

His hand tightened on the knob of the door. "You said it was infatuation."

"I was wrong."

"No, you were right." He jerked the door open. "You don't love me."

"I'm not letting you run away from me," she said softly. "You made sure I came to this island and now I'm staying." She paused. "With you, Jordan. And when you leave, I'm leaving with you. That's how it is going to be from now on. You and me—together."

"You don't know what you're saying."

"You'll see. You once said I was strong. Well, you haven't seen anything yet."

"Oh, Sara. . . ." He shook his head and strode out the door.

A faint smile was on Sara's lips as she turned away and moved toward the adjoining bathroom.

It had begun.

Nine

Sara made a face at the image reflected in the mirror of the bureau. When she had packed to come to Penny's island, she'd had no idea she would need anything but sturdy, utilitarian clothing and this plaid wool caftan was meant for warmth and not glamour. But at least the emerald green color was good with her hair and eyes. Judging from Jordan's resistance earlier today, she'd probably need every edge she could muster this evening. She turned away from the mirror and moved toward the door.

The hall and living room were deserted as she started down the stairs but Jordan entered the house before she reached the bottom step. He hesitated, gazing at her warily. He abruptly turned away and started down the hall. "I'll go make dinner."

"It's already made. I threw together a beef stew while you and Cam were working on the radio." She followed him down the hall. "Where's Cam?"

"He took the launch to Santa Barbara to check out the radio." He opened the door to let her precede him into the kitchen. "We can't get a line patched to Penny's apartment. He should be back late tonight or early tomorrow morning."

"What seems to be the problem?" Sara asked as she began dishing up the stew from the pot into the earthenware bowls she'd set out on the countertop.

"We don't now. The phone just rings off the hook. We're probably being connected to the wrong number. Penny has to be there. She told me she'd be working at home so that she'd always be in touch." He paused. "She's a good friend to you."

"Yes, she is. Though I may have to come to a new understanding with her after this little fandango." She picked up the bowls and turned around. "She shouldn't have . . ." She inhaled sharply and forgot what she was saying as she met his gaze. He wanted her. It was there in the sensual curve of his lips and the intensity with which he was looking at her. Her hands were suddenly trembling and she tightened her grip on the bowls. She smiled with an effort as she moved across the room toward the oval mahogany table. "I've made enough for three. I hope you're hungry."

"Not very." He dropped down in a chair and spread his napkin on his lap. "You didn't have to do this. I could have done the kitchen duty."

"'Why?" She put one of the bowls in front of him on the place mat. "If I still considered myself a prisoner, I'd let you wait on me hand and foot, but the situation has changed." She went around the table and set her bowl down on the place mat before seating herself opposite him. She grinned mischievously. "If anything, I consider you my prisoner. Though I'll make every effort to make your captivity enjoyable."

"How . . . interesting." He didn't look at her as he picked up his spoon. "You didn't, by any chance, manage to sabotage the radio to get rid of Cam?"

"Nope." She began to eat. "But I do regard it as a sign from on high that my cause is just."

"You sound like a medieval knight."

"I feel a little medieval and I've always thought it unfair that women weren't permitted to become knights. I think you have a few dragons to be fought and why shouldn't I help?" She met his gaze and added deliberately, "Though if you'd rather I be Queen of the May than vassal, I'm agreeable to that too."

His fingers tightened on the spoon. "I'm not agreeable."

"I know. That's one of the dragons." She put down her spoon with great care. "That and the Jonah complex you seem to have acquired. It's enough to discourage a woman."

"You don't appear to be discouraged."

"That's because this is too important to me to let anything stand in my way." She paused. "*You're* too important."

"I wasn't all that important to you two days ago."

"Yes, you were." Sara held up her hand to stop him as she opened his lips. "I know. I know. You probably have a right to be suspicious of this sudden reversal on my part. Do you think this is easy for me? You manipulated me and I resent the hell out of that. When I realized I loved you, I knew I had to put that anger aside if we were going to make our relationship work. But I didn't think I'd have to fight you too." She stood up. "But if that's the way it has to be, then I'll have to do it. Put down your spoon. You're just toying with that stew anyway."

"What?"

She came around the table, took the spoon away from him, and put it down on the table. "You're evidently not going to do justice to the main course, so you might as well have dessert." She plopped down in his lap and put her arms around his neck. "Relax." She nestled her cheek against his chest. "You're stiff as a board."

"That doesn't surprise me." His voice was muffled in her hair. "Will you please get off me?"

"No." His heart was thundering in her ear and her embrace instinctively tightened around him. "I like it here. Put your arms around me."

"No."

"Okay, I don't want to be pushy. It would be nicer if you held me, but this is all right too." She unbuttoned the top three buttons of his shirt and pressed her lips to his chest as she'd been tempted to do earlier today at the pier. She buried her lips in the dark wiry hair and then turned her head to lick delicately at his nipple. She felt a shudder run through him. "Don't you think it's pleasant?"

"About as pleasant as a night in an iron maiden."

She laughed softly. "I'm not a maiden and I'm certainly not made of iron and you've always found nights with me pleasant in the past." She rubbed her cheek back and forth on the hard, warm flesh she had bared. "Or so you've told me."

"Sara . . ." His voice was strangled. "I can't take much more of this."

"Good. Have I seduced you?"

He didn't answer. His chest was rising and falling with every breath and she could feel the hard column of his manhood pressed against her bottom. Heavens, the man was stubborn, Sara thought ruefully. "No? But I believe I could seduce you if I went just a little further, don't you?" She nibbled gently on his nipple.

His heart gave a double beat and he made an involuntary motion as if to take her in his arms. He stopped and his arms dropped again to his sides.

She sighed as she slowly straightened and buttoned his shirt. "I don't think you're ready to be seduced, so I'll back off. I don't want to be accused of using you again."

"I told you I didn't mind your using me."

"But I mind. I think we're going to have to revamp your philosophy on the value of using people." She cuddled closer to him again. "Let's just try to give to each other instead. There's so much I want to give you, Jordan. Love, trust, children . . ." She could feel him relaxing, the tension gradually ebbing from his locked muscles. "Do you realize we've never discussed children? Would you like a son?"

"Maybe." His arms slipped around her with the greatest care, holding her as if she would break if he exerted the slightest pressure. "I never thought about it. It was always just you. I think I'd rather have a daughter."

"That pleases my feminist sensibilities but it surprises me. I thought most men wanted a mirror image of themselves."

"Maybe most men like what they see in the mirror better than I do. I'd rather look at a reflection of you." His palm touched the sleek curve of her hair with uncharacteristic awkwardness. "You could never reflect anything that wasn't bright and beautiful."

She swallowed to ease the tightness of her throat. "We'll take turns then. One of each. The next question is, when do we start? Next year?"

"I don't care. Whatever you want," he said absently, his hand tangling and playing in her hair. "Whenever you—" He broke off as pain tightened his features. "I can't, Sara. It won't work. I couldn't stand—" He lifted her off his lap and stood up. "I've got to get out of here."

"It's a small island. I'll only follow you. You burned your bridges when you let Cam take the launch." She tried to smile. "Now there's no way you can escape me."

"Cam will be back tomorrow."

"But he's on my side. I bet he'll make himself so unobtrusive, we won't even know he's on the island."

"Sara." Jordan's face was tormented. "Don't do this. You're tearing me apart."

"Then give up," she whispered. "Please give up, Jordan. We've both made so many mistakes. Don't make another one."

"You're the one who's making a mistake," he said hoarsely. "You don't know what's good for you."

"But that's what I'm trying to find out." She paused. "But I know neither of us is going to discover anything by running away. You should have learned by my example."

"I'll *hurt* you, dammit. I won't mean to do it but I will." He whirled on his heel and strode out of the kitchen. A moment later she heard the door slam behind him.

Sara drew a shaking breath as she turned away and began to clear the table. For a first foray it hadn't gone badly. Jordan was too tough to cave in without a battle, but he was obviously fighting himself as well as her. Surely he couldn't hold out long. Oh, dear, what if he did hold out? She wasn't accustomed to playing the aggressive vamp, and the entire situation made her most uneasy.

She carried the dishes to the sink and set them on the counter. There was no reason to be uneasy, she told herself firmly. As long as Jordan loved her, she was the one in control. She shook her head as she noticed how her hands were trembling. If she was so in control, why was she scared to death she would do something wrong?

Sara was sitting curled up on the couch reading a Danielle Steel paperback when Jordan came back to the house several hours later. She glanced up, smiling casually. "You look as if the north wind just blew you into the hacienda. Is it chilly?"

He eyed her warily. "A little."

"You've been out a long time. You'd better take a hot shower."

"I will." He hesitated. "I'm going to bed."

She gazed up at him innocently. "I'm so glad you shared that with me. Sleep well."

He frowned. "Alone," he added deliberately.

She nodded serenely.

He started up the stairs.

"Tonight," she said softly.

He stopped, but didn't turn around. "I beg your pardon?"

"I decided to beat a strategic retreat," she said. "I think you need a chance to get your breath and mull things over. You're quite safe from my advances tonight."

"That's good." His tone was oddly flat as he resumed climbing the steps.

"I decided tomorrow was soon enough." Her gaze returned to her book. "Good night, Jordan."

She kept her gaze fastened on the page she was reading as she heard him mutter a curse beneath his breath. A moment later the door of his room slammed behind him.

Sara chuckled. It was a good thing the doors of Penny's hacienda were strong and the hinges sturdy. They had certainly gotten a thorough workout since she and Jordan had arrived at Penny's "sanctuary."

"You're not going to like it." Cam strode down the gangplank toward the pier, where Jordan was waiting. "I sure as hell didn't."

"You couldn't get the radio fixed?"

"It wasn't broken. We were being connected with Penny Lassiter's apartment. She just isn't answering."

Jordan tensed. "You're sure?"

Cam nodded. "Jeanine, the supervisor at the telephone company and I are now bosom buddies." A reminiscent smile tugged at the corners of his lips. "And what a truly magnificent bosom she has. I wish I'd had more time to—"

"That's not good," Jordan interrupted Cam's discourse on the mammary attributes of the voluptuous Jeanine. "Penny Lassiter suggested the patch herself, and she wouldn't just flit off somewhere without getting word to us."

"I didn't think she would either, so I had Jeanine contact the apartment manger and she persuaded him to go up and check. No one answered the bell."

"Damn!"

"That's how I felt. Particularly, after I called *World Report* and found she'd told them she'd be working at home and that they hadn't been able to reach her since one o'clock yesterday afternoon."

"Where the hell could she be?"

"There's no use getting uptight," Cam said calmly. "We'll find out. I asked Maria to handle the matter personally and she'll—"

"Who the devil is Maria?"

"Maria Garcia. She's a detective first class with the Santa Barbara police department. Didn't I mention I'd gone to see them?"

"No," Jordan said dryly. "You seem to have been very busy." He shouldn't have been surprised. He knew that beneath Cam's good-humored facade was a steel-sharp mind and a drive that equaled his own. "And what's Maria going to do?"

"She's contacting the San Francisco police department and requesting them to gain entrance to Penny Lassiter's apartment and see if they can find any clues as to where she went. She'll radio me as soon as they report back to her. Satisfactory?"

Jordan shook his head ruefully. "My God, Cam, if you formed an army of all your conquests, you could rule the world."

"I've never liked the world *conquest*," Cam said with distaste. "I like women and I'd never want to beat them down." An impish smile suddenly lit his face. "And besides, with an entire army of women I'd be too busy to rule the world."

Jordan chuckled and felt a little of his tension leave him. Cam had always had that effect on him since the time they were teenagers together. Cam's warmth had always seemed to be able to lighten any burden. "Point taken. Did your detective tell you when she'd be likely to call?"

"No. Do you want me to stay with the launch until she contacts us?"

Jordan hesitated before shaking his head. "I'll stay here. You go back to the hacienda and keep Sara company. Try not to tell her anything about Penny that will worry her."

"I don't think it's my company she wants. My God, Jordan, forget Bandora. This is what you've wanted since the first day you met Sara. Reach out and take it."

Jordan started across the pier toward the gangplank. "I'm through taking from her. She'll be better off without me."

"Isn't that her choice?"

"No, it's mine."

Cam stood watching him resignedly as Jordan crossed the deck. "When shall I come down to relieve you?"

"Don't come. There are blankets and an inflatable mattress here. I'll bunk down in the cabin."

"Is that really necessary?" Cam asked, surprised.

Jordan glanced back over his shoulder. "I'm not sure, but I don't like not being able to get in touch with Penny. This is the only place on the island that's accessible by helicopter or launch, and it might be best to mount a twenty-four-hour guard."

"But why not alternate watches? Suppose I come down at sundown and relieve you and then you can—"

"No! I'll do it myself." He tried to temper the sharpness of his tone. "You just stay with Sara."

"But will Sara stay with me?" Cam asked, gazing after him. Jordan didn't answer, and Cam shrugged resignedly as he started along the pier toward the rocky shore.

The breeze was chill and crisp, and the crashing surf pounded against the launch, causing it to buck and heave against its moorings.

The deck shivered beneath the rubber soles of Sara's tennis shoes as she moved toward the cabin. The deck wasn't the only thing that was shivering, Sara thought. The temperature had plummeted since this afternoon and each breath she expelled sent mist into the air.

"Who's there?"

Sara blinked as the powerful beam from Jordan's flashlight momentarily dazzled her. "Do you mind turning that off? I'm seeing black spots in front of my eyes and this moonlight makes it almost as bright as day anyway."

Jordan muttered something under his breath and switched off the flashlight. "Go back to the house. It's freezing out here."

"Cam said you had blankets," she said cheerfully as she strolled toward him. "And body heat is even better. I'm sure we'll make out. Did you eat the supper I sent down with Cam?"

"Yes." He frowned. "This is crazy, Sara."

"I agree. But what else can I do? If Mohammed refuses to come to the mountain . . ." She shivered. "I hope you still have some coffee left in that thermos I stuffed into the picnic basket. We're going to need it later."

"Later? You need it now. Why didn't you wear a jacket?"

"I was afraid it would get in the way." She smiled as she stopped before him. "I told you that you couldn't run away from me." She stripped off her white cable-knit sweater and dropped it on the deck. "It's time for the seduction to start."

She was naked to the waist, her breasts full and beautifully taut in the moonlight.

He stared at her, feeling an aching tightening in his groin. "Dear heaven, Sara, put your sweater on. You've got to be freezing."

"You're right, I've got goosebumps."

His gaze was fixed in compulsive fascination on her naked breasts. "I can see you do."

"Perhaps if you'd put your hands on me I'd be warmer." She took a step closer and took both his hands in her own. They were cold, hard, and a shiver trembled through her that was only half due to the cold as she imagined his hands on her flesh. "Hold me, Jordan." She put his palms on her naked breasts. "Keep me warm."

His hands tightened on her breasts, cupping and squeezing, and suddenly the cold was gone. Heat streaked through her in rivulets of flame. Her lips parted to allow more air into her constricted lungs. "Yes that's it. Help me to—"

"Damn!" Jordan wrenched his hands away. "I'm as crazy as you are. In another minute I'd have had you rolling around naked on this blasted deck." He bent down and snatched up her sweater before his hand encircled her wrist and he pulled her into the cabin. It wasn't really a cabin at all, Sara noticed, but little more than a shallow area beneath the controls of the launch. But at least they were sheltered from the dampness and the wind. Jordan dropped her sweater beside a blanket-covered mat to pick up a dark blue woolen throw and drape it around her naked shoulders. Then he knelt by the picnic basket and rummaged for the thermos. "Sit down. I'll get you some of that coffee."

"I'd rather have you."

He froze, then stood up, holding out a plastic cup filled with steaming liquid. "This will help."

"Jordan . . ." She took the cup and sipped the hot coffee. "As a seductress I'm obviously a washout. If I'd been good at this, we *would* have been rolling around on that deck."

"You were damn good at it," he said dryly. "The temperature was the only thing that saved me."

"That's reassuring." She took another sip of coffee. "You know, we've never made love on a boat before."

"And we're not going to do it now."

She sat down on the inflatable mattress, clutching the blanket with one hand, and crossed her legs Indian fashion. "You don't like the idea? I think all the bucking and rolling might be quite erotic." She smiled up at him. "Why don't we try it?"

"Will you stop this, Sara?" Jordan asked roughly as he sat down across from her. "Just finish your coffee and get the hell out of here."

"I can't. I'm trying to beguile you."

He froze. "Beguile? You said something about me beguiling you right after you were hurt."

"Did I? I vaguely remember something about that, but I was pretty much out of it."

"You asked why I had beguiled you. I felt as if you'd stabbed me."

Sara experienced a sudden rush of pity. "I was out of my head. I didn't know what I was saying."

"No, you were right. I *had* deceived you."

She suddenly moved to kneel before him, her eyes glowing softly in the moonlight. "Will you stop whipping yourself? I don't even know if that was what I meant. You know, *beguile* has a meaning other than deceit." Her index finger touched his cheek with infinite gentleness. "It also means to tempt or charm. You do beguile me, Jordan, and you always will. Even when all your dark corners are lit and I learn everything about you, you'll still have that magic for me. If I wasn't sure of that, do you think I'd be risking a rejection on this scale?" She made a face. "It isn't all that good for my ego."

He moved his head and her palm was suddenly pressing against his lips. "You don't have any ego."

She laughed. "Maybe I have a few dark corners left for you, too, if you think that. I most certainly do have an ego, and what's more, I can be very competitive." She tapped his lips with mock sternness. "So don't think I'll tolerate any of your shenanagins with other women."

"There's never been any other woman." His voice was low. "Not really. With other women it was only sex but you were . . ." He trailed off and briskly tucked the blanket more tightly around her. "Finish your coffee and then run back to the house, where it's warm."

She shook her head. "Not unless you come too." She drained the last of the coffee and set the plastic cup back in the picnic basket. "Which isn't a bad idea. We'd be much more comfortable in my bed."

He shook his head.

"Your bed?"

He shook his head again.

She sighed. "Okay. Then it's this hard deck and nature in the raw. You're a very difficult man, Jordan." She stretched out on the mat and tried to make herself comfortable. "At least come and hold me."

"Go back to the house."

She lifted herself on one elbow to meet his gaze.

"No way." There was a steely edge to her tone. "I'm never going to sleep away from you again. Your bed is my bed."

"Your bed is likely to be in the hospital if you try to sleep out here in this damp cold," he said in exasperation. Then, when she didn't answer, he gave a low exclamation and moved to lie next to her. He snatched two blankets from the pile beside the mat and spread them over her before gathering her in his arms to share the heat of his body. "This is a mistake."

She burrowed closer. "No, it's just right. It feels . . . sweet. I'm almost glad you didn't let me seduce you."

He was rigid against her. "Are you?"

"Uh-hmm. This may be even cozier. I don't remember a time when we've just lain together without making love. I probably shouldn't have tried to seduce you anyway, because that's not what this is all about. I guess I figured I needed all the help I could get, so I tried to use the same weapon to manipulate you as you did me. You have a perfect right to resent me doing that."

"I don't resent it."

"That's good. Now we can just lie here and hold each other and talk." She paused, waiting. "Why aren't you talking to me?"

"I can't think of anything to say." He was surprised he could put two words together, with her nipples poking so saucily against his chest. He tried to think of something, anything, to take his mind off the softness of her. "Go to sleep."

"Hmm, that will probably be nice too." She relaxed against him as confident as a small child and nestled her head against his shoulder. She smothered a yawn. "The movement of the boat is kind of soothing, isn't it?"

"You think so?" He didn't feel at all soothed. He felt exasperated and tormented and horny as hell. And tender. He found the tenderness sweeping through him was submerging all the other emotions. He sighed and drew her closer. "This isn't going to do you any good. I'm not changing my mind, Sara."

"It's bound to do some good." She yawned again. "If only to show you that I'm acting as I mean to go on. Besides, I'm enjoying this. Aren't you?"

The pleasure was exquisitely bittersweet but he couldn't deny it existed. Tomorrow he would have to think of a way to keep her at a distance but tonight, perhaps, it would do no harm to embrace the pleasure and pain of her nearness. "Yes," he said thickly. "I'm enjoying it." His hand reached up to stroke the silkiness of her hair. "I like this."

"Do you find me beguiling too?" she asked drowsily. "In the nice way, I mean."

Beguiling, enchanting, his life, and his torment. His lips feathered her temple. She gave a soft murmur of pleasure and he knew she was almost asleep. "In the nicest possible way."

"Good."

Jordan gazed into the darkness for a long time after Sara had drifted off to sleep. She was fragile, almost weightless in his arms, but tenderness and desire twisted inside him like a burning cork-screw. It was all very well to say he would accept half a loaf, but he wasn't accustomed to refusing to take what he wanted, and he wanted Sara like a man dying of thirst craved water.

Water. His mother's face twisted and contorted, her lips cracked and bloodless.

He shuddered and his arms unconsciously closed with iron force around Sara. She murmured a protest in her sleep and he forced himself to relax his grasp. Lord, he had hurt her again. He would always hurt her, whether he intended to or not. He would grab and hold and suffocate and in the end it would be the same.

Sara was wrong. They had no chance for a future together. There was only tonight.

Ten

"What are you doing?" Sara raised herself on one elbow to look at Jordan standing by the radio. How satisfying it was to wake up and find someone you loved nearby, she thought contentedly. She hadn't realized how much she'd missed that pleasure in the last eighteen months.

He switched off the radio and turned toward her. "A message just came though from Santa Barbara," he said quietly. "Did you hear it?"

She shook her head as she sat up and rubbed her eyes with her fists. "I just woke up. Was it important?"

"Yes, it was important. And definitely unsettling." He stood there frowning thoughtfully for a moment before coming to a decision. "We're getting out of here." He picked up her sweater from the deck beside the mat and tossed it to her.

"Run up to the hacienda and tell Cam to bring our suitcases down here right away. I'll have the launch ready to go when you get back."

The underlying urgency in his tone brought her wide awake. "What's wrong? Did Penny call?"

"No." He paused. "Penny's disappeared."

Her eyes widened with shock. "Oh, no!"

"She may be okay," he said quickly. "The police didn't find a—"

He didn't have to complete his sentence, Sara thought in horror. He had been going to say they hadn't found Penny's body. "Tell me what's going on. There's more, isn't there?"

"There didn't seem any sense in worrying you," Jordan said gently. "We only had suspicions."

And Jordan had been trying to protect her again, Sara thought in exasperation. "Tell me."

"We weren't able to contact Penny, so we arranged for the police to gain entrance to her apartment. They found signs of a hurried departure." He paused. "And something else. The stub of a Greyhound bus ticket."

Sara felt as if an icy hand had closed around her heart. "Kemp."

Jordan nodded. "The possibility is there. The police seem to think he studies his victims carefully and would have known Penny was your friend as well as your employer. If Kemp was clever, he'd try to use her for information or hostage purposes."

"He's not clever." Sara pulled on her sweater to try to ward off the chill that was creeping through her. "But he does have a certain animal cunning.

He *is* an animal. If you'd seen the pictures of what he did to those poor women. Oh, Lord, Penny!"

"I hope to heaven the police are wrong," Jordan said. "But we can't help Penny from here, and it's you we have to worry about now. You're his primary target, and he may have forced Penny to tell him where you are."

"Not Penny. She'd die before she'd—" Sara broke off, and covered her mouth with a trembling hand. "He'll kill her, Jordan. Maybe he has already."

"We don't know that." He pulled her to her feet. "But we do know this island isn't safe for you any longer. Go back to the house and tell Cam we have to leave."

"All right," she said numbly. She left the cabin and moved dazedly toward the gangplank. She heard Jordan's footsteps on the deck behind her as he followed her. Then the sound of his footsteps stopped abruptly and he gave a low exclamation. She turned to look at him and saw that he was gazing out to sea, vigilance tensing his every muscle. "Is something wrong?" She followed his gaze and saw a small sailboat on the horizon.

"No," he said quickly. He crossed the distance between them in three strides, then his hand was beneath her elbow, propelling her down the gangplank. "It's just a fisherman. Hurry and get to Cam."

She found herself hurrying down the pier, swept away by the urgency in his voice. She glanced back as she reached the shore. He was still standing there watching her. "Hurry," he said again. "Get to Cam."

She nodded and started at a half trot up the hill.

Get to Cam.

The words repeated over and over in her mind. Even through the bewilderment and horror that clouded her thinking she was aware there was something wrong with his phrasing.

She reached the summit of the hill and started down the other side. Why hadn't Jordan told her to go for Cam instead of get *to* Cam? It was as if he didn't mean her to fetch Cam but was sending her to Cam for safety.

The fisherman.

Her pace faltered as a bolt of sheer panic flashed through her. How could she have been so thick-headed? What fisherman would risk this wild surf in a flimsy sailboat? But Kemp would risk it. Kemp wouldn't care; nothing would stop him.

Jordan would die for you, Penny had said.

"No!"

Sara whirled and tore back up the hill. Her breath was coming in painful gasps as she reached the summit and paused to look down at the pier. The sailboat was tied up but there was no sign of an occupant. She couldn't see Jordan either. Her gaze desperately searched the pier before moving to the shore.

Steel glittered in the sunlight.

Two figures were struggling on the rocks— Jordan and the man at whom she had stared in fascinated horror during those months in that New York courtroom. A sob of terror broke from her throat as she started running down the hill. Kemp had a knife. What if he killed Jordan before she managed to reach them?

He'd die for you.

No, Jordan mustn't die. She had to stop Kemp before he killed him. But she was still so far away.

"'Kemp!" she screamed. "I'm here!"

Did he hear her? The two men were still struggling, and as she watched, Kemp's knife was creeping toward Jordan's throat.

She screamed his name again. "Kemp!"

He heard her! He lifted his head and saw her.

"Sara, don't!" Jordan's desperate voice.

Kemp hesitated, his knife poised over Jordan's throat. Then he was off Jordan and running toward Sara.

She hesitated. Which way? Fear and uncertainty froze her in place.

"Run, Sara!" Jordan was on his feet, dashing after Kemp, trying to reach him before the man reached Sara. He mustn't do that, Sara thought frantically. Kemp might reverse his moves any second. She turned left and ran down toward the shore, trying to lead Kemp away from Jordan.

The rocks were so slippery. She had fallen once. What if she fell now? Kemp was right behind her. She could hear him cursing. . . .

Tears were streaming down her cheeks. She didn't want to die. Was this how those other women had felt before he plunged his knife into their flesh? What if she fell?

"Bitch. Bitch. Bitch." Kemp's litany pounded on her from behind. "Die, bitch. You're going to die. You and that other brown-haired whore on the boat. Bitch. Bitch."

She slipped. Recovered her balance. Kept on running.

A hoarse snarl of triumph behind her. He sounded closer.

He *was* closer. Running faster.

"No!" Jordan's shout. "Kemp, you bastard. Me!"

Jordan meant Kemp was to take his life instead of hers, she realized through a panicky haze. He must know Kemp was going to catch her or he wouldn't sound so frightened. Kemp was too fast. He wouldn't stop. He never stopped.

A startled scream pierced through her raw terror. Was she screaming? No, it was someone else. Jordan? She risked a frantic glance over her shoulder. Jordan had tackled Kemp and, as she watched, Kemp lost his balance and toppled into the sea with a tremendous splash.

She stopped, her breath coming in shuddering gasps.

Kemp was struggling wildly, his arms thrashing to keep himself above the surface. His pale blue eyes protruded from his chalky face as his gaze fastened on her with hatred. "Bitch," he shouted. His mouth filled with water and he choked and gasped, but as soon as he could breathe he shouted it again, "Bitch!"

He was jerked beneath the surface of the water as if pulled by the tentacles of a giant octopus.

He didn't come up again.

Jordan was beside her, enfolding her with trembling arms. "Sara! My God, why? He almost killed you."

Her arms slid around him and held on to him with all her strength. She burrowed her head into his shoulder. "He's dead, isn't he? The riptide . . ."

"He's dead." Jordan's voice was trembling as much as his body. "It could have been you in the water. It could have been you." His lips were pressing frantic kisses on her temples and cheeks. "You almost fell . . ."

She released him and turned to look at the place in the water where Kemp had disappeared. "I'm glad he'd dead," she whispered. "I'm glad he can't hurt anyone else. All those poor women . . ." She stiffened as the memory of Kemp's words returned to her. "Penny." She turned and started back to the pier at a dead run. "We've got to find out if he's hurt Penny!"

"What do you think?" Penny touched her cut, swollen lip gingerly as she gazed ruefully at her bruised face in the hand mirror. "Do I look like Muhammed Ali or Sugar Ray Leonard? I think Leonard. Ali never got this beat up in his entire career."

"Don't joke." Sara took the hand mirror and laid it facedown on the kitchen table. "I feel guilty enough knowing that it was my fault Kemp did this to you." She gently applied salve to Penny's cut lip. "I was so afraid he'd murdered you. When we found you tied up on that sailboat, you looked absolutely beautiful to me."

Penny made a face. "You looked pretty good to me too after looking at nothing but Kemp's ugly mug for almost forty-eight hours."

"How did it happen?"

Penny shrugged. "He was more crafty than we all thought. He knew the New York police had set him up and he decided to make sure he didn't fall into the trap. He showed up at *World Report* pretending to be a maintenance man and scouted around until he found out you'd left town and I'd been the one Mac told to handle getting you away. Then he paid a visit to my apartment and managed to get a key from the super by masquerading as an inspector from the gas company, sent to check on a reported leak."

"How could he do that? Your apartment usually has great security."

"His face," she said simply. "He has the most ordinary face I've ever seen. He looks like the man who picks up your garbage or checks you out at the grocery store. He was very convincing whatever role he played." She tried to smile. "However, he didn't appear quite so ordinary to me after he'd worked on me for a while. He wanted to know where you'd gone and became quite upset when I told him to go to hell. Unfortunately, when he searched my apartment he found the receipt from the helicopter service."

"Dammit, Penny, you should have told him where I'd gone and let me take my chances."

"It wouldn't have done any good," she said wearily. "Then he would have taken great delight in slitting my throat. Until he was sure he knew where you were, I was safe. The phone practically rang off the hook that first day, and I was hoping Jordan would realize something was wrong and be on guard." She looked at Sara inquiringly. "Where is Jordan? I haven't seen him since the two of you brought me up to the house."

"He's down at the launch. He and Cam are radioing the police to tell them about Kemp." Sara stepped back and gazed at Penny's face in discontent. "That's all I can do. You really should see a doctor."

"No," Penny said as she quickly stood up. "I'll be fine. I'm going to take a shower and wash my hair before I radio Mac." She turned away with a shiver. "Kemp was . . . I don't know if I'll ever feel really clean again."

"Thank you, Penny," Sara said quietly. "I know the words are inadequate, but they're all I have to give you. I only hope someday I can repay you."

"I don't want to be repaid, it was my choice to help you." Penny said, glancing back over her shoulder. "And I'd do it again. I learned something very important in the last forty-eight hours."

"What?"

Penny smiled crookedly. "That there are no sanctuaries except those we have within ourselves."

Sara watched Penny leave the kitchen, then turned back to replace the salve in the open first-aid kit on the table. It was over. It was difficult to believe the deadly threat that Kemp represented was in the past. He had haunted her for such a long time.

"How is she?"

Sara turned to see Cam standing in the doorway, his face clouded with concern. "She says she's fine but it's not true. I think that monster did more damage to her mind than he did to her body." She closed the first-aid kit with a firm click. "Penny's a survivor. It will take time, but she'll work her way through it."

"And you'll be there to help her," he said gently.

"You bet I will. All the way." She turned to smile at him. "Why didn't Jordan come with you?"

"He's getting the launch ready to leave. He told me to come and tell you—"

Panic zipped through her. "Leave!" Her eyes were suddenly flashing with anger. "Hasn't there been enough trouble without Jordan deciding this is the time to sail off into the sunset?"

"Sara, I didn't say—"

She wasn't listening to him. "I can't believe it. Well, I'm not about to let him go off and . . ." The words trailed behind her as she ran from the room.

• • •

"You're not leaving." Sara strode down the pier, her hands clenched into fists at her sides. "Do you hear me, Jordan? I'll be damned if I'll let you leave me."

Jordan turned to face her, startled. "How's Penny?"

"She could be better," Sara said curtly. "I don't want her to be alone right now, so I can't be bothered to chase you halfway across the world. You'll just have to stay with me."

A faint smile touched his lips. "How militant you're being. What if I don't choose to stay? Will I be chained to your wrist like a diplomat's briefcase?"

"If necessary." She blinked back tears of anger and exhaustion. "I'll do anything I can to keep you here. It's stupid of you to even think of leaving me when you love me. And you do love me. Why don't you admit it?"

"I love you," he said obediently.

"You're so damned frightened that I'm going to be hurt—" She stopped and tried to steady her voice. "Well, if you don't stay with me, I'll get Penny and Mac to give me the most dangerous assignments they can dredge up. Beirut, investigative reporting, drug running."

The smile disappeared from Jordan's face. "The hell you will."

"And if they won't do it, I'll quit and go to work for a magazine that will."

"Suicide assignments?" Jordan asked grimly.

"Not suicide. I'd try my best to stay alive. I told you I wasn't like your mother." She took a step closer, her eyes glistening like misty emeralds as she gazed up at him. "I'm strong enough to stand alone, but I'll be damned if I want to. So I'm going to exert a little muscle. The only way you're ever going to know I'm moderately safe is if you're by my side." The tears that had been brimming were now running down her cheeks. "Penny said the only sanctuary was within ourselves, but that's not true. If you love someone, that can be a sanctuary too. *You're* my sanctuary, and my safety, and the place that gives me pleasure and strength and—" Her voice broke. "Do you think I'll ever let you take that away from me?"

"Evidently not." Tenderness softened the hard planes of his face, and the way that he was looking at her was beautiful. He took her into his arms. "You're a very formidable lady."

"Only when I'm driven crazy by a stubborn, muddled man who—"

His fingers on her lips stemmed the tirade. "Stop maligning me. I was *not* leaving you. I only thought we should get Penny off the island to see a doctor. You've won."

She went still. "I have?"

"If you call living the rest of your life with a man like me any kind of victory. You'll probably regret it next month or next year."

"I'll never regret it." Her gaze searched his face. "Why?"

"Kemp," he said. "I'd never seen you that close to death, even when you fell and hit your head. It was something I'd always dreaded, my worst nightmare, and there it was before me. I knew then that if you lived, I'd never be strong enough to let you go again. I'd always have to be wherever you were, right next to you to try to help you and keep you safe." He paused before adding haltingly, "And happy. Lord, I'll try to keep you happy, Sara."

"Sanctuary?" she asked softly.

"If that's what you want, that's what I'll try to be for you. Life won't be easy for you. I'll probably still be possessive and jealous."

"And loving."

"Oh, yes." He nodded, taking her into his arms with enormous tenderness. "Always loving. Is that compensation enough?"

Joy rippled through her like a glowing sunlit river. "Compensation?" She kissed him gently. "Jordan, loving is all that matters. Don't you know that?"

He nodded, his smile as joyous as her own. "I think you're beginning to teach me. I hope you'll still think so fifty years from now."

"I will," she whispered as she gazed up at him lovingly. "You can count on it."

THE EDITOR'S CORNER

June is certainly a month for gorgeous, passionate, independent, loving, tender, daring, remarkable heroines! With three of the six women of the month being redheads, you can be sure to expect fireworks! Magdelena is washed right into her lover's arms in the rapids; Lux falls into her lover's arms with a giant teddy bear; Meghan has risky plans for her man; Candace finally wants to give all; Lacey's free spirit needs taming; and Randy learns to surrender . . . All this and a whole lot more in our June LOVESWEPTs. Read on to learn about each book and the wonderful heroes who fall in love with these six fabulous heroines.

In **CONFLICT OF INTEREST** by Margie McDonnell, LOVESWEPT #258, Magdelena Dailey, our heroine with long, wild hair, is rescued from a Colorado river by Joshua Wade who steals a passionate kiss as his reward. Joshua is a sweet seducer, a man made for love. Magdelena needs quite a bit of convincing before she changes her plans and lets a man into her life again, and Joshua is up to the challenge. There's no resisting his strong arms and tender smile, and soon Magdelena is riding the rapids of love!

Lux Sherwood is a raven-haired beauty in **WARM FUZZIES**, LOVESWEPT #259, by one of our perennial favorites, Joan Elliott Pickart. All Lux needs is one of her very own creations—a giant teddy bear—to get Patrick "Acer" Mullaney's attention. Acer is a star quarterback with a serious injury that's keeping him out of the game—the game of football, that is. He's definitely strong enough to participate in the game of love, and here's just a taste of what Acer has to say to Lux:

> "My needs run in a different direction. I need to kiss you, hold you, touch you. I need to make love to you until I'm too exhausted to move. I don't want to be just your friend, Lux. I won't be."

(continued)

What's a woman to say to such a declaration? Lux finds the right words, and the right actions in **WARM FUZZIES**!

We're so pleased to bring you our next LOVESWEPT for the month, **DIVINE DESIGN**, #260, by first novelist Mary Kay McComas. With a redheaded heroine like Meghan Shay and her daring scheme, we're certain that Mary Kay McComas is headed for LOVESWEPT success! Her hero in **DIVINE DESIGN** isn't bad either! Who can resist a long, tall Texan whose eyes gleam with intelligence *and* naked desire. Michael Ramsey has all the qualifications that Meghan is looking for—in fact he's too perfect, too good looking, too kind, too wonderful—and she can't help but fall in love, and that's not part of Meghan's plans. Ah, the best laid plans . . .

Barbara Boswell delivers another moving love story with **BABY, BABY,** LOVESWEPT #261. By popular demand, Barbara brings you Candace "Barracuda" Flynn's love story. And what a love story it is! Candace wants a second chance with Nick Torcia, but Nick is wary—as well he should be. Candace burned him once, and he isn't coming back for more. But something has changed. Precious new babies have brought them both an understanding of love. Still, Nick needs to lay the past to rest. Here's a sample of the intensity of their encounter:

"Why did you lead me on, Candy?" Nick demanded, his onyx eyes burning into hers.

"Not for revenge," she whispered.

"Then why, Candy?"

Her heart seemed to stop beating. He was so close to her, close enough for her to feel the heat emanating from his hard, masculine frame.

"Nick." His name escaped from her throat in a husky whisper, and she tried to move closer. Desire, sharp as a stiletto, sliced through her. She wanted to lose herself in his arms, to feel his hot, hard mouth take hers. She gazed at him with undisguised yearning.

But Nick wouldn't let her close the gap between them. He held her wrists, controlling her movements and keeping her anchored in place. "Tell me, Candy."

Tyler Winter is the man who tames Lacey Lee Wilcox's free spirit in **FOR THE LOVE OF LACEY**, LOVESWEPT #262, by Sandra Chastain. Tyler is a renaissance man—an artist, businessman, and an absolutely irresistible hunk! Is

(continued)

he a flirt or really a man Lacey can trust her heart to? Tyler showers her with kisses, gives her wildflowers, and takes her on picnics, but still Lacey is afraid of losing her heart. With just a little more convincing our heroine loses her fears and listens to her heart:

"Tyler," turn me loose," Lacey ordered.

"Nope," he said, moving his mouth toward hers.

Not again, she begged silently. Too late. She was being kissed, thoroughly kissed, and there was no way to stop him. Tyler finally drew back and grinned down at her with undisguised joy.

"Tyler," she protested, "you don't know what you're doing."

"You're right, and it's been a long time since ignorance felt so good. Kiss me, Lacey."

In **HAWK O'TOOLE'S HOSTAGE** by Sandra Brown, LOVESWEPT #263, Randy Price can't believe what's happening to her. It's 1987, yet she's just been abducted by a masked man on a horse! No, this is not part of the old west show she was watching with her son. Who is this masked man? And why does he want Randy? Hawk O'Toole is an Indian Chief with very good and honorable reasons for kidnapping Randy Price, but he doesn't plan on the intense attraction he feels toward her. She's his hostage, but fate turns the tables, and he becomes her slave. Love has a way of quieting the fiercest battles as Randy and Hawk find out.

Happy Reading! Remember to look for The Hometown Hunk Contest next month—it's your big chance to find the perfect LOVESWEPT hero!

Sincerely,

Kate Hartson

Kate Hartson
  Editor
LOVESWEPT
Bantam Books.
666 Fifth Avenue
New York, NY 10103

ENTER
THE DELANEYS, THE UNTAMED YEARS
MISSISSIPPI QUEEN RIVERBOAT CRUISE
SWEEPSTAKES
W I N
7 NIGHTS ABOARD THE LUXURIOUS
MISSISSIPPI QUEEN STEAMBOAT
including double occupancy accommodations,
meals and fabulous entertainment for two

She's elegant. Regal. Alive with music and moonlight. You'll find
a Jacuzzi, gym, sauna, movie theatre, gift shop, library, beauty
salon and multi-tiered sun deck aboard…plus a splendid dining
room and lounges, beveled mirrors, polished brass, a Grand
Saloon where big band sounds soothe your soul and set your feet
to dancing! For further information and/or reservations on the
Mississippi Queen and Delta Queen' Steamboats
CALL 1-800-458-6789!

Sweepstakes travel arrangements by
RELIABLE TRAVEL INTERNATIONAL, INC.

Whether you're travelling for business, romance or adventure,
you're a winner with Reliable Travel International!
CALL TOLL FREE FOR INFORMATION AND RESERVATIONS
1-800-645-6504 Ext. 413

**MISSISSIPPI QUEEN RIVERBOAT CRUISE SWEEPSTAKES
RULES AND ENTRY FORMS ALSO APPEAR IN THE
FOLLOWING BANTAM <u>LOVESWEPT</u> NOVELS:**

THE GRAND FINALE	**MAN FROM HALF MOON BAY**
HOLD ON TIGHT	**OUTLAW DEREK**
*CONFLICT OF INTEREST	***DIVINE DESIGN**
*WARM FUZZIES	***BABY, BABY**
*FOR LOVE OF LACEY	***HAWK O'TOOLE'S HOSTAGE**

and in

**THE DELANEYS, THE UNTAMED YEARS:
COPPER FIRE; WILD SILVER; GOLDEN FLAMES**

*On sale week of May 2, 1988   SW10

OFFICIAL DELANEYS, THE UNTAMED YEARS
MISSISSIPPI QUEEN' RIVERBOAT CRUISE
SWEEPSTAKES RULES

1. NO PURCHASE NECESSARY. Enter by completing the Official Entry Form below (or print your name, address, date of birth and telephone number on a plain 3"x 5" card) and send to:

> Bantam Books
> Delaneys, THE UNTAMED YEARS Sweepstakes
> Dept. HBG
> 666 Fifth Avenue
> New York, NY 10103

2. One Grand Prize will be awarded. There will be no prize substitutions or cash equivalents permitted. Grand Prize is a 7-night riverboat cruise for two on the luxury steamboat, The Mississippi Queen. Double occupancy accommodations, meals and on-board entertainment included. Round trip airfare provided by Reliable Travel International, Inc. (Estimated retail value $5,500.00. Exact value depends on actual point of departure.)

3. All entries must be postmarked and received by Bantam Books no later than August 1, 1988. The winner, chosen by random drawing, will be announced and notified by November 30, 1988. Trip must be completed by December 31, 1989, and is subject to space availability determined by Delta Queen Steamboat Company, and airline space availability determined by Reliable Travel International. If the Grand Prize winner is under 21 years of age on August 1, 1988, he/she must be accompanied by a parent or guardian. Taxes on the prize are the sole responsibility of the winner. Odds of winning depend on the number of completed entries received. Enter as often as you wish, but each entry must be mailed separately. Bantam Books is not responsible for lost, misdirected or incomplete entries.

4. The sweepstakes is open to residents of the U.S. and Canada, except the Province of Quebec, and is void where prohibited by law. If the winner is a Canadian he/she will be required to correctly answer a skill question in order to receive the prize. All federal, state and local regulations apply. Employees of Reliable Travel International, The Delta Queen Steamboat Co., and Bantam, Doubleday, Dell Publishing Group, Inc., their subsidiary and affiliates, and their immediate families are ineligible to enter.

5. The winner may be required to submit an Affidavit of Eligibility and Promotional Release supplied by Bantam Books. The winner's name and likeness may be used for publicity purposes without additional compensation.

6. For an extra copy of the Official Rules and Entry Form, send a self-addressed stamped envelope (Washington and Vermont Residents need not affix postage) by June 15, 1988 to:

> Bantam Books
> Delaneys, THE UNTAMED YEARS Sweepstakes
> Dept. HBG
> 666 Fifth Avenue
> New York, NY 10103

- -

OFFICIAL ENTRY FORM
DELANEYS, THE UNTAMED YEARS
MISSISSIPPI QUEEN' RIVERBOAT CRUISE SWEEPSTAKES

Name _____

Address _____

City _____ State _____ Zip Code _____

SW10